Heart Trouble

SHARON MAYNE

WITHDRAWN
FOR SALE

NORTHUMBERLAND

Accession No. | Class No.

COUNTY LIBRARY

MILLS & B
ETON HOUSE, 18-
RICHMOND, SURREY TW9 1SR

All the characters in this book have no existence outside the imagination of the Author, and have no relation whatsoever to anyone bearing the same name or names. They are not even distantly inspired by any individual known or unknown to the Author, and all the incidents are pure invention.

All rights reserved. The text of this publication or any part thereof may not be reproduced or transmitted in any form or by any means, electronic or mechanical, including photocopying, recording, storage in an information retrieval system, or otherwise, without the written permission of the publisher.

This book is sold subject to the condition that it shall not, by way of trade or otherwise, be lent, resold, hired out or otherwise circulated without the prior consent of the publisher in any form of binding or cover other than that in which it is published and without a similar condition including this condition being imposed on the subsequent purchaser.

First published in Great Britain in 1992
by Mills & Boon Limited, Eton House, 18-24 Paradise Road,
Richmond, Surrey TW9 1SR

© Sharon Moehn 1992

ISBN 0 263 78064 3

Made and printed in Great Britain

1

WELCOME TO WILD, Wonderful West Virginia, the highway sign read. Alone in her sports car, Ashby White allowed herself an unladylike snort of derision as she downshifted to round a mountain curve. "Wild," she'd agree with, but she begged to differ about the "wonderful" part. And she certainly disagreed with the state's other slogan, Almost Heaven.

Her memories of Grant County, West Virginia, bore a closer resemblance to hell. A tar-paper shack, its yard littered with the rusted hulks of cars stripped for parts to keep a battered pickup running . . . faded clothes handed down from sisters and the Salvation Army . . . watery potato soup thinned to feed ten hungry mouths . . . and dolls made from flour sacks and dried corn husks when she'd craved a store-bought princess dressed in satin and lace.

She'd fled all that seventeen years ago. Why was she returning? she asked herself for the umpteenth time. The sight of the blacktopped road before her seemed to fade and in its place she saw the worn, tired faces of her parents and heard their gentle voices urging their eight children to study hard in school, to better themselves. And they had, every one of them.

Her parents were dead, she reminded herself, and her vision cleared. Her brothers and sisters were scattered from Alaska to Florida. But still the restlessness filling her at the approach of her thirty-fifth birthday had drawn her back to her roots. Why? The question reverberated through her head.

Her friends back in Washington, D.C. had accepted her explanation of a working vacation as logical and reasonable, like all her actions. But she couldn't lie to herself.

After seventeen years of single-minded determination, she'd reached her goal and now felt lost. Why?

She exhaled loudly and tapped her long fingernails on the black leather-bound steering wheel, then admired the pale pink of her nail polish, the same shade that adorned her equally well-manicured feet in their open-toed, high-heeled sandals. Never again would her fingernails know the sooty grime from filling a coal-burning stove nor her feet the squish of mud through her bare toes.

So, what was she doing back in Appalachia? Longing to escape the question, she pressed harder on the accelerator and closed her mind to everything but the feel of her sports car hugging the twisting road that wound through the rolling green of the Allegheny Mountains.

She slowed reluctantly when a sign announced the town limits of Hickory and warned her to lower her speed. A boarded-up mine shaft—mute testimony to the town's origins—clung to the side of the mountain. A hodgepodge of houses and trailers lined the paved switchbacks and rose in rows up the steep hillside so that the porch of one overlooked the roof of another.

Ahead of her, on the other side of town, she saw the glint of sunlight on the metal span of a bridge crossing the Potomac River back into Maryland. Drawn by the sight, she deliberately passed the turnoff to the scenic Highland Trace Highway, her tentative destination.

She'd get gas and cross that bridge. She'd tell her friends she'd changed her mind. She had no reason to be back in West Virginia.

FROM HIS SEAT on the bench beneath the shaded porch in front of the Hickory General Store, Wade Masters narrowed his eyes and watched the woman in the red Porsche convertible coming toward them. A flashy package, he thought, in her look-at-me sports car. A nice change of scenery. He didn't mind accommodating her by staring.

"Thar's a purty piece," his companion on the bench commented, as the Porsche turned into the gas station across the road.

Wade repressed a chuckle. Age and arthritis might have slowed his grandfather, Coot Rogers, but his eyesight was still sharp.

"Nice car." Wade leaned back and folded his arms over his chest, then stretched his legs across the wooden porch to rest his feet on the railing.

"Wasn't talking about the car," Coot grumbled, shifting his skinny shanks on the hardwood bench.

"Those are out-of-state license plates. She's only passing through."

"She's coming this way."

Wade had already noticed. "Looks like you'll have a customer. Their pop machine is broken." He'd watched her gas up, then considerately park her car away from the pumps before using the rest room and trying to buy a pop. She'd spoken to the station attendant, who had pointed in their direction as she paid him.

Coot was right; she was a pretty piece. Her white jumpsuit fit over slender curves, and he had a feeling he wouldn't be disappointed in the view when she came close enough for him to see her face clearly.

Aware of the two men watching her, Ashby carefully looked to her right and her left before slowly crossing the highway. She remembered the boredom of country afternoons all too well. She wasn't about to provide them with entertainment by tripping and making a fool of herself.

The light tap of her high heels against the pavement sounded unnaturally loud in the quiet of the small town sleeping in the spring sun. Her self-consciousness grew beneath the silent scrutiny of the two men as she crunched across the graveled parking area in front of the store, then climbed the wooden porch steps. But she returned their stares with one of her own as she removed her sunglasses.

Choosing to ignore the man whose long legs stretched across the porch and blocked her path, Ashby nodded at the small, grizzled man next to him.

"Howdy." Coot stood and hitched up the straps of his denim overalls. "What can I do for you?"

"The man across the street said you . . ." her attention caught by the display in the plate-glass window behind the men, Ashby's voice faded ". . . sold sodas."

A handcrafted chair dominated the exhibit. Two tall saplings served as the back supports, their boughs left untrimmed to reach toward the ceiling. Lower down, tree limbs bent into right angles formed the arms and front legs, while forked branches created a backrest. The seat was made of strips of black cowhide woven in a herringbone pattern. It looked, Ashby decided, as if a throne had grown out of a tree.

"What would you like?" the old man asked. "The hummers sure look purty in a window, and the crystal prisms catch the light real good. Make rainbows on a sunny day."

Only then did Ashby notice the hummingbirds and other glass ornaments hanging from the tree boughs, but she barely spared them a glance. Mesmerized by the artistry and originality her training recognized in the crafting of the chair, she didn't answer.

The style had its origins in the rustic tradition of Adirondack camp furniture, but the lines of this chair were light and graceful compared to the dark, heavy, more primitive appearance of the antiques. The bark had been stripped and the wood sanded and polished to a pale, smooth finish that made her fingers itch to stroke it.

"The chair," she finally murmured.

The other man's feet slid off the railing and hit the porch with a thump. Ashby turned to him. He was a good foot taller than her own five foot two and the width of his shoulders seemed to fill the small porch, but she squared her own shoulders and stiffened her back to stand as straight and tall as she could.

She'd always hated being short, even though her mother had softened the description to "petite." Her three-inch heels made her almost five-and-a-half feet tall, but she still had to lift her chin to meet the man's eyes.

"The chair is not for sale." Neither a smile nor a trace of apology softened his flat statement. Ashby wanted an explanation, but an indefinable sense of power in his steady gaze seemed to pin her in place and keep her silent. Unable to break her strange paralysis, she returned his stare.

People didn't have emerald eyes except in books, she mused absently; the color in real life was hazel. But not a speck of brown deepened the startling green of these eyes set beneath thick brows in a rugged face bronzed by the sun. Jet black hair swept back from his high forehead and brushed the collar of his faded shirt.

He had a hawklike nose and high cheekbones that made her wonder if he was of American Indian ancestry. He was certainly not city-bred, of that she was certain. Nor was he a stranger to physical labor. She couldn't believe that the muscles straining the thin cotton of his blue T-shirt were created in a gym any more than that tan came from a spa.

His arms were folded across a broad chest, each hand resting on a rounded biceps. His fingers were long, squared and blunt. Everything about the man hinted of strength and she suddenly understood the primitive criteria for the selection of a mate. In a quest for sheer survival, this man would be her first choice.

"Is there anything else I can do for you?" he asked.

Startled out of her reverie, Ashby blinked up at him. A grin played at the corners of his mouth and the gleam in his green eyes flirted with her, suggesting things he could do for her that had nothing to do with his furniture and everything to do with his masculinity.

So much for the country boy and her theory of physical labor, she thought wryly, ignoring a quiver of feminine pleasure. The man was smooth and sophisticated, his baritone voice sounding cultured in contrast to the older man's country twang.

He'd caught her gawking like a schoolgirl, but years of imitating good breeding—which to her meant hiding one's personal reactions—stood her in good stead. "No, but I'd like to know why I can't buy the chair," she shot back.

Coot cackled and Wade grinned. He couldn't help it. Coot's odd laugh was infectious and he had to admit the woman had more spunk than he'd expected. Pleased that he'd so readily accepted her rebuff, Ashby smiled.

"The chair was a gift," Wade said. Her face, as he'd anticipated, didn't disappoint him. Despite the casual elegance of her white jumpsuit and the pink scarf tied like a turban around her head, she had a gamin's smile. Her features were small and delicate, like her figure. Blond tendrils peeked out from under the scarf. She reminded him of an elf except that her big blue eyes met his directly rather than shyly or mischievously.

"Do you have any other pieces?" Uncomfortable beneath that green-eyed examination, Ashby turned to the older man.

"No." Wade answered for his grandfather.

"Do you know the artist?"

"Artist?" Wade grinned. "He's just a guy who makes crazy furniture for friends." He turned to Coot. "I've got to go. Tell Mom I'll see her tomorrow."

Intrigued, Ashby watched him leave. One stride of his long, denim-clad legs and he was off the porch without using the steps. Three more and he'd reached a four-wheel-drive Ford pickup with a camper top. Although it was a recent model, its mud-spattered tan exterior showed hard use on dirt roads.

When he was gone, she turned back to the older man. "He made the chair."

Coot hooked a thumb under each of the shoulder straps on his overalls and studied her. "Yep," he said. "But if he says it's not for sale, it's not. He's a stubborn cuss, just like his grandpaw."

"Why?" she asked, following him when he turned to lead the way into the store. He favored his right leg and limped slightly, she noticed, but otherwise walked as erectly as his grandson.

"The whys and the wherefores, you'd have to ask him. What kind of pop would you like?" Coot lifted the lid of an old cooler that predated the modern, stand-up vending machines, and Ashby peered inside.

"When in West Virginia, what else but Mountain Dew?" She dropped some coins into the slot, lifted out her selection and looked around. The old store with its creaking hardwood floors, potbelly wood stove, aged brass cash register and squat, gallon-size jars full of colorful hard candies transported her back to her childhood.

"Got any Fireball candy?" she asked, surprising herself, as well as the older man.

Coot's eyebrows rose, but he moved behind the counter and unscrewed the lid of a jar filled with balls of red candy. "How many?"

Ashby spied a lunch-size paper bag and picked it up. "A bagful. I haven't had a Fireball in years. Are they as good as they used to be?"

"Try one and see." Coot handed her one and she stuck it into her mouth, then nodded as the rich flavor of hot cinnamon burst upon her tongue.

"Cost more than a penny these days," he warned as he filled the bag. Ashby shrugged her disregard for the price, not wanting to speak around the hard ball in her mouth. "You a West Virginny girl?" he asked as he weighed the bag of candy on a rickety scale.

She nodded, aware that for the first time she felt a trace of pride rather than shame at the admission as she paid for the candy. She liked the directness of the wizened old man and wanted him to like her. He had the same green eyes as his grandson, or rather, his grandson had his eyes. But the younger man hadn't inherited his size from his grandfather. The man before her wasn't much taller than she.

She pushed the candy to the side of her mouth, where it protruded against her cheek. "From the other side of the mountain, near Weathersfield."

The bell on the door tinkled as a small, plump woman with graying hair entered. "Lunch," she told Coot, then smiled pleasantly at Ashby as she set a wicker picnic basket on the counter. "Would you care to join us?"

Ashby retreated a step, polite refusal on her lips. Hospitality was a trademark in the Appalachians as well as in the deep South, but she doubted that these people had much to share. The store was neat and tidy, the exterior freshly painted, but she couldn't believe it ran much of a profit in such a small town.

"The girl wants to buy Wade's chair," Coot said to the woman and Ashby's farewell froze on her lips. He picked up the basket. "This here is Millie Masters, my daughter and Wade's mother. I'm Coot Rogers, his grandpaw."

Yes, there was a third set of those startling emerald eyes, Ashby noticed as she introduced herself and followed the two to the back of the store. Coot pushed through a screen door and they stepped out onto an open deck. The ground dropped away behind the building so that they stood level with the treetops. He plopped the basket onto a picnic table and waved at the women to sit down.

Ashby hesitated, swallowing the last of the Fireball. "I really don't want to intrude on your lunch, but I'd like to talk to you about the furniture."

"Plenty to eat, and Millie's the best damn cook in Grant County. Sit." Ashby sat and Coot delved into the basket.

"Where is Wade?" Millie asked.

"He done took a good look at this little lady and run off like a scairt jackrabbit."

"Oh, really?" Millie smiled and cocked an eyebrow at Coot's confirming cackle.

Mystified by their humor, Ashby looked from one to the other, but neither offered an explanation. Coot plunked a paper plate down in front of her as Millie opened plastic containers. "I'm afraid the chicken is leftover cold, but the biscuits are hot," Millie said, passing out the food.

"Buttermilk biscuits hot from the oven?" Ashby eyed the flaky rolls appreciatively. "And Southern-fried chicken, I bet!"

"She's from Weathersfield." Coot winked at Millie. "Knows a good meal when she sees one."

"It's been a while." Ashby didn't want to give them the wrong impression. They both seemed very pleased that she was a native of their state. "I live in Washington, D.C., now."

Coot shrugged. "You kin take the girl outta the country, but you cain't take the country outta the girl."

Ashby chose not to mention how hard she'd fought to do exactly that as she dug into the meal, the likes of which she hadn't had in years. Home-canned pickles, beets, peaches and three kinds of jam added to their feast.

"I run an art gallery in Georgetown," she explained, after praising the food. "And I plan to do a folk-art exhibit in the fall. That chair is exactly what I'm looking for."

Maybe she did know what she was doing, she thought with relief. The idea of such an exhibit had come to her more as an excuse to fulfill the strange urge to return to her roots than as a true goal. But it really wasn't a bad idea, especially if she could get that chair for the focal point.

"It's not a large gallery, but it would give your son's furniture some excellent exposure." Deliberately, Ashby played on a mother's pride as she turned to Millie.

"Wade says he won't sell," Coot told his daughter. "I warned her he's a stubborn cuss."

"I don't give up easily, either," Ashby added, when Millie smiled but remained silent.

"You'll need a place to stay, then," the older woman said after another moment of thought. "We live just down the road. Why don't you room with us?"

"Oh, I couldn't impose. Surely there's a motel...."

"All full up," Coot said. "Seein' as it's the Fourth of July and a three-day weekend, city folk come a-runnin' to the country for a look at nature."

"The Highland Trace Highway," Ashby mused aloud. Apparently she hadn't been the only one to see the article in the travel section of the *Washington Post* touting the scenic attractions along state Route 55. Not sure what was drawing her back to West Virginia, she'd decided to take the drive and stop whenever or wherever the whim caught her. But after seeing Wade's chair, she was more interested in her idea of a folk-art exhibit than in sight-seeing.

"And there's a fair with craft booths in Clairmont, three miles south," Millie added persuasively. "We have more than enough room and if you stay with us, you can stop there tomorrow." She smiled. "And Wade wouldn't be able to avoid you, either. Matter of fact, why don't you take the rest of this chicken to him? Catch him on his own ground and he'll have no place to run."

Coot cackled. "No time like the present!"

Ashby didn't question her good fortune or the look Coot exchanged with Millie as they gave her directions to Wade's mountaintop farm. She couldn't take them up on their hospitable invitation, but she wasn't about to turn down the excuse they'd provided for her to meet the furniture maker again.

She had no trouble finding the nearby town of Clairmont, but didn't bother stopping to look for a motel. She was too eager to confront Wade. The uncertainties that had plagued her during her four-hour drive from Georgetown had vanished, to be replaced by a more familiar sense of purpose. Once she explained who she was and how she could help Wade make a career of his furniture, she was sure he'd jump at the opportunity to sell.

She watched her odometer closely. She didn't trust herself to spot the cairn of rocks Coot had described by the entrance to Wade's farm. Instead, she followed Millie's instructions to travel two miles and take the first road on the left.

She soon wished she'd asked how far up that dirt road Wade lived. Her low-slung Porsche barely made it to the first gate. Ruts and rocks threatened to rip out its bottom. No wonder Wade drove a four-wheel-drive truck, she fumed, pulling over as far as she dared and exiting the car.

But her high heels didn't fare much better than the Porsche on what she could no longer, by any stretch of the imagination, call a road. She leaned against a tree and bent to remove her shoes. Stuffing them into the picnic basket, she picked her way gingerly around cow piles and trudged upward. Back in West Virginia and barefoot already, she realized disbelievingly.

The sun grew hotter, the basket heavier. Beads of perspiration gathered under her scarf and her sunglasses slipped down her nose. Disgustedly, she stuck the glasses in her pocket and used the scarf to wipe away the trickle of moisture between her breasts. Without looking in a mirror, she knew the despised curls she straightened so laboriously with a blow dryer every morning were returning with a vengeance. But she couldn't bear the warmth of the scarf on her head any longer and it joined her sunglasses in her pocket.

"Five foot two, eyes of blue . . . cutesy-cutesy-cutesy coo," she remembered her father singing. The older she got, the more she hated the word cute. How was she going to convince Wade Masters that she was a knowledgeable art-gallery owner when she looked like a *cute*, if sweaty, kid fresh out of college? And where in hell was his house?

The sound of a *woof* drew her attention from the path and her mouth, already dry, went drier at the sight of a black bear loping down the hill straight toward her. She looked frantically to her right and left. Nothing but bushes. Where was a nice tall tree when she needed one?

"You cain't outrun a bear," her father had warned when she was a child. "Freeze, if you cain't climb a tree." Her eyes closed and she clutched the wicker basket to her chest. Then her eyes popped open at the realization that the basket had food in it. She dropped it, retreated a step and closed her eyes again, feeling her arms rise up to cross her chest in a protective reflex. Her heart pounded against her ribs as if struggling to run without her.

"Samson, heel!"

Ashby opened her eyes at the sound of a human voice, although she barely comprehended the words. The animal paused and looked back over its shoulder. She followed its gaze and saw Wade Masters descending the hill. The bear looked back at her and she swore it licked its chops, but it remained where it was.

"I said heel!" Wade strode closer and the animal ran to his side.

"A bear! You keep a bear for a pet?"

"Samson isn't a bear, you idiot. He's a dog, a New-foundland."

Ashby flushed as she looked more closely at the huge, furry black animal. Its squared muzzle did not resemble the longer, narrower snout of a bear. "He startled me," she muttered as Wade halted in front of her. Why, she wondered, wasn't her heartbeat steadying now that the danger was over?

"Good. He's supposed to scare off trespassers."

Ashby swallowed an angry retort in hopes of getting on his good side, although she was beginning to doubt that he had one. She indicated the basket at her feet. "Your mother sent you some food, since you didn't stay for lunch."

Wade mumbled something she didn't catch and bent to take the basket. Ashby kept her eye on the dog. Bear or not, she thought he looked as if he wanted to eat her for dinner.

"Coot seemed to think I scared you away," she added sweetly, hoping to pierce Wade's cool self-possession.

"Thank you for delivering the basket." He ignored her comment. "Now you're free to leave." He turned back in the direction he'd come. He knew exactly what his family was up to and he wasn't going to have anything to do with it. He'd come to terms with his solitude; why the hell couldn't they?

"What?" Ashby couldn't believe he'd so rudely dismissed her. "I nearly ruined my car and walked all the way up here and you tell me to leave? The least you could do is offer me a glass of water! It's hot walking in this sun, in case you haven't noticed."

Wade swung around slowly, his gaze rambling over her. He saw wide blue eyes, tousled blond curls, fair cheeks reddened by heat and temper. He dropped his gaze lower, noting how the thin fabric of her jumpsuit clung to her moist skin. A grin inched across his face. "You're a cute little bundle, but I guess you already know that." Better than the usual female specimens his family persisted in thrusting at him.

"Cute? I *hate* that word!" Ashby resisted the urge to stamp her foot. Why couldn't the guy have the decency to invite her to the cool shade of his home, where they could have a civilized conversation about his furniture? "And whether I'm cute or not has nothing to do with why I'm here. I brought that basket because I want to talk to you, and I am *not* leaving until I do."

Wade covered the distance between them in one long stride. "Correction," he snapped as he set the basket back on the ground. "That's exactly why Coot and my mother sent you up here!"

"I don't know what you're talking about."

"Do you mean to tell me that you make a habit of following strange men to their homes?" He loomed over her. "Don't you know you could get hurt?"

Without her high heels, the difference in their heights was great enough for him to block the sun. Standing in his shadow, she felt small and defenseless . . . and very aware of how isolated they were. Instinctively she retreated a step. The erratic beat of her heart no longer had anything to do with anger, but everything to do with the cold clutch of fear.

2

A SMALL SMILE softened Wade's stern expression as Ashby edged away. A victorious smile, she thought and realized that rather than intending her harm, he intended to intimidate her into leaving.

"Just what ulterior motive do you think Coot and Millie had in sending me up here?" she demanded, halting her withdrawal and crossing her arms beneath her breasts.

Wade's smile dropped into a scowl. "To get us together. They're a pair of matchmakers. They can't get it through their thick skulls that I choose to be alone." He took a step toward her, then stopped, planting his feet far apart and jamming his hands into his back pockets.

The stance threw his shoulders back and jutted his hips forward aggressively, but Ashby no longer felt threatened. Instead, an errant feminine part of her admired the pure masculinity of the pose. She shook her head and raked her fingers through her short curls in a fruitless effort to smooth them back. As if, she thought wryly, she could make sense out of this situation by repairing her appearance.

All she wanted from the man was his furniture, and he thought she wanted him! She felt like laughing, but didn't dare.

"Regardless of your family's motives," she said crisply, "I accepted their suggestion to come here for reasons of my own, which, I assure you, have nothing to do with infringing on your bachelorhood. If you would be kind enough to offer me a seat out of this sun and a glass of water, I'll explain them." Pretty rational, she complimented herself, even if her curls still felt like corkscrews.

"I warn you, I've been living up here, alone—without a woman—for the past two years." And I like it that way, he tacked on silently, to deny the bitterness that had crept into his thoughts.

"Which is the way you want it, so I have nothing to be afraid of. Right?"

Wade cocked an eyebrow in acknowledgment of her sarcasm and stepped aside, a sweep of one hand inviting her to precede him. "'Step into my parlor said the spider to the fly.'" She was one determined little lady, he thought with grudging admiration. He'd hear her out, then send her on her way. He had no other choice.

"Thank you." Her courtesy mocked his surly invitation. She stalked past him as he picked up the wicker picnic basket and whistled for his dog.

Samson hadn't wandered far. Ashby swallowed nervously as the big black dog joined them, then relaxed as he wagged his tail and lumbered up the path. She followed him up the mountain, while Wade lagged behind her. When she topped the rise she saw a two-story log cabin. Ivory roses tinged with peach flanked the front steps and mingled with the glossy green of rhododendron bushes lining a redwood deck. The leafy canopies of dogwood and redbud trees sprinkled shade around a large lawn dotted with the purple and yellow of tiny violas.

"It's lovely," she exclaimed, unable to keep the surprise out of her voice.

"Did you think I lived in a tin shack?"

"A cave wouldn't have surprised me."

Wade moved abreast of her reluctantly. He'd enjoyed watching the slight sway of her hips as she walked in front of him. But he grinned down at her, amused by her sarcasm. She smiled, too, then glanced away.

"Did you build the cabin yourself?" she asked as they reached the flagstone path leading to the front steps. In her mind's eye, she could see him shirtless, his damp chest gleaming in the sun as he swung the ax, felling trees to build a home.

"I bought the kit, then put it together."

Ashby blinked as her mental image crumbled. This was the twentieth century, she reminded herself, not pioneer days. But putting a home together from a kit was still no easy task. The men she knew would have hired a crew. She was still impressed. This man worked with his hands. Obviously he had strength. Competence. Skill.

He led the way up the steps and opened the screen door. "Have a seat." He indicated the porch swing. "I'll be right back."

Samson flopped down by the door and Ashby eyed him warily. She would have liked to follow Wade into the house to see if he'd made any other furniture. "Nice boy," she murmured, edging toward the swing, "nice Samson." The dog huffed and closed his eyes.

Relieved, Ashby sat down and stared at the view. A tree-lined river snaked through the small town spread out below the mountain. Clairmont, she guessed. Fluffy white clouds hovered over the rounded, green-clad peaks rolling away into the distance. A strange pang pulled at her heart. Nostalgia? she wondered as she remembered lazy summer afternoons spent picking out shapes of animals in such clouds with her brothers and sisters.

"Beer or iced tea?" Wade called from inside the house.

"Tea." Ashby swung back and forth gently and thought of her tiny, brick-walled yard in Georgetown.

Wade returned, handed her the tea, then propped one hip up on the porch railing opposite her. He popped the top of a beer can, raised it to his lips and drank. Ashby sipped at her tea. The ridges around the lip of the glass told her it was an old jelly jar.

"What happened to your shoes?" Wade asked. Her toenails, he noticed, were painted the same pale pink as her long fingernails. And those fingers bore no rings. He again swigged at his beer. But what did that matter? He could see those pink-tipped hands against his skin, could feel their soft touch . . . but he couldn't see them puttering in the garden beside his.

Ashby dropped her gaze to her dusty feet and blinked, surprised that she'd forgotten she was barefoot. "My sandals are in the basket. I didn't want to turn my ankle on the cow path that serves as your driveway." Embarrassed, she pulled her legs up onto the swing and sat Indian-fashion, tucking her feet out of view beneath her knees.

Wade shook his head. "Never understood how anyone can sit like that." Stupid, idle conversation, he realized. Why didn't he make her get to the point and send her on her way? Because he liked looking at her. With her short blond curls tousled and no longer covered by the scarf, her crisp jumpsuit rumpled from her long walk and her feet bare, she almost looked like she belonged on that porch swing. Except for the long fingernails and flashy pink-and-white hoops dangling from her ears—those reminded him that she belonged to another world, a world he'd been forced to abandon.

"Your legs are too long," she said and he looked at her blankly, having forgotten what they were talking about. "To sit Indian-fashion," she explained.

"You noticed the differences between us." His gaze pointedly skimmed over her curves.

Ashby flushed. This man discomfited her. Why? She couldn't put her finger on a reason. She was accustomed to handsome men, rich men, powerful men. Lawyers, politicians, lobbyists, executives, doctors, diplomats, scientists. The art world of Georgetown attracted them all. So why did this country boy who wasn't a country boy make her feel so ill at ease?

Because he was no boy, the answer rapidly followed the question. He was man, all man. Not some dandy in a three-piece suit who depended on words to make his living. No streak of silver lightened his temples, yet she was certain he matched, if not exceeded her nearly thirty-five years.

"Why won't you sell me your chair?" she asked bluntly. *That's it*, she thought with satisfaction. *Get down to business*.

Wade's smile faded into a frown. "So they told you I made it."

Ashby nodded, although his statement was more an observation than a question. "My name is Ashby White and I own an art gallery in Georgetown," she said crisply. While she hadn't wanted Coot and Millie to think her pretentious, she wasn't about to mince words with Wade. He had to realize what she was offering him in order to take her seriously. "And I'm planning a folk-art exhibit. Your furniture would show quite well—"

"Ashby?" Wade interrupted. "Interesting name." He ignored the rest of the information she gave him. "That's a fairly common surname in this part of the country."

"It was my mother's maiden name. I'm from Weathersfield." She offered the information in hopes that her West Virginia roots might please him as they had Coot. They didn't.

Wade threw his head back and laughed—a full, rich sound that seemed to imprint itself on her mind. "You're a country girl?" No wonder Coot and Millie had sent her to him. Of course, with their hearts firmly planted in Hickory, they'd overlooked the fact that this woman's heart was firmly entrenched in the city. "What's the saying? 'You've come a long way, baby!'"

"Yes, I have." Ashby was curt. She was proud of her success, but coming from him, the statement sounded more like an insult than a compliment. "And as I said, I own an art gallery in Georgetown and I'd like to exhibit your work."

"I'm not interested." Wade slipped off the railing, stood and set the beer can down on a nearby table, then turned his back on her.

"People would pay a pretty penny for such unique furniture."

"I don't need the money."

"Everyone can use more money."

"I have everything I need." His lips twisted in a cynical smile as he turned his head toward her. "Except, according to my family, a woman. Are you sure you're not volunteering for the position?"

A flare of excitement skittered along her nerves and Ashby gripped the jelly jar with both hands to hide a sudden tremor. *Don't touch that question,* she ordered herself. *He's only trying to rattle you.* "Why make the furniture if you won't share it?"

"One, I enjoy making it." He returned his gaze to the mountain-rimmed horizon. "It's a hobby and gives me pleasure. Two, I do share it. With friends, not strangers." He stared down at her, his expression unyielding. "Are you ready to leave yet?"

"I haven't finished my tea." He was rude, Ashby decided, absently tapping her fingernails against the glass she held, and he was hiding something. He spoke too quickly and hadn't met her eyes until asking if she was ready to leave. "Why do you have a chair in Coot's store, if you won't sell it?"

"He put it there. Thought it would attract tourists' attention."

"Could I see any other pieces you've done?"

"No. Drink your tea."

Ashby scowled. "You've lived alone too long. Your manners are deplorable." Why, she fumed, wouldn't he give her offer the serious consideration it deserved?

"Does it offend you to drink out of a jelly jar? Sorry, I don't have any Waterford crystal."

"I wasn't referring to the jar." She drank the last of her tea to demonstrate.

"Oh, you mean *I* offend you?" He spread one hand across his wide chest, an expression of dumbfounded amazement on his face. "Then why don't you get in that fancy car of yours and drive back to your big city? I didn't invite you here. Why should I be a good host?"

She *had* intruded on his privacy, Ashby admitted, but how could he be so blindly obstinate that he couldn't recognize what she could do for him? And his snide reference to her car added fuel to her increasing irritation. The Porsche, she knew, was both flashy and extravagant. But after ten years of skimping and scraping to save enough money for her gallery, she'd owed herself that luxury and wasn't about to apologize for it.

She stood and slammed the jar down onto the railing next to him. "Because I did your mother a favor by bringing you your lunch!"

"We already went into why she sent you." Wade hooked his thumbs into the pockets of his jeans and leaned back on the railing. His grin was smug and triumphant.

Ashby silently counted to ten. He was, she decided, the most infuriating male she'd ever met. Also the most masculine. She skittered away from that thought and rallied her defenses. "If you don't care about the income your furniture could provide for yourself, you could at least think of your mother and grandfather. Coot shouldn't have to work in that store."

Wade threw his head back and laughed. "Coot owns—and loves—that store." He straightened, looming over her. "Are you really thinking of me or my family? Aren't you thinking of the money you want to make from my furniture?"

"Of course I'd earn a commission," Ashby said tightly, clinging to her temper as she glared up at him. "I'm a businesswoman. But you'd have more to gain. I can give you more exposure than you could possibly acquire on your own. Most artists would jump at the chance to have their work on exhibit in Georgetown."

"But I'm not an artist."

"Then what are you?"

Wade grinned at the blunt question. "I told you, just a guy who makes crazy furniture for friends. Come on, I'll drive you back to your car." His long fingers wrapped around her arm and propelled her down the porch steps.

"My shoes," Ashby protested, reminded she was barefoot by the heat of the sun-warmed flagstone walkway on her soles and snatching at the excuse to delay her departure.

Wade released her and turned to go back to the house. Ashby followed hard on his heels, determined to sneak a peek at the inside of his home.

"Stay," he commanded as though she were Samson. She glared at his departing back as he entered the house, then tried to peer through the screen door into the dim interior. But he returned far too quickly, his large frame blocking her view.

She stepped back as he pushed through the door. Her shoes looked like toys dangling from his hands. She took them from him, but when she bent to put them on, he cupped her elbow.

"You can do that in the truck." He hurried her around the house, where she saw the tan vehicle parked in front of a large red barn.

His workshop? Ashby wondered, even as she reconciled herself to her imminent departure. Not that she was about to give up. She'd retreat for now and find a room, then rethink her strategy. She wasn't going to leave West Virginia without Wade's furniture. All she had to do was figure out what made the man tick, then hit him with the right blend of persuasion and incentive. He was a stubborn mule of a man, but she hadn't attained her current success by running from a challenge.

She smiled as Wade called to Samson and ordered him inside the barn, confirming her suspicion that the red building contained valuables. She'd be back to get a look inside that barn, she promised herself, barely noticing the neatly tended garden full of green sprouts next to it.

"Allow me to get the door for you," Wade said with exaggerated courtesy as he returned to her side and remembered her low opinion of his manners. It was rude to rush her away, he knew, but she represented what he could no longer have in life. And he didn't like the reminder. He was content with his life, if not deliriously happy. And it was far preferable to the alternative.

Ashby eyed the high step into the truck with misgiving, but bit her tongue rather than ask Wade for help. She tossed her shoes inside, then grasped the door with one hand and the side of the truck with the other as she lifted her foot to the running board. Before she could haul herself up, Wade's hands circled her waist and lifted her.

Her blood pressure shot up alarmingly. His touch was not good for her. Her heart quivered like a bowstring, her palms felt as moist as those of a schoolgirl about to receive her first kiss, and the heat burning in her cheeks told her she was blushing.

She ducked her head and busied herself by strapping on her high-heeled sandals as Wade climbed behind the steering wheel. The man was an eccentric recluse, she reminded herself, not suitable for her at all. But why didn't the touch of the sophisticated men she dated have the same effect on her as his?

ASHBY HADN'T ANSWERED that question by the time she'd reached Hickory and turned onto the gravel road leading to Coot and Millie's home. She'd stopped at all three motels in Clairmont and not one had a vacancy. With the same friendly solicitude that Coot and Millie had exhibited, several of the motel owners had called inns in other towns for her, but there wasn't a room available within a fifty-mile radius.

"These here hills are getting to be quite the tourist spot," one woman had told her proudly. Ashby had smiled and nodded, but thought the problem stemmed more from a lack of lodgings. She should have made a reservation in advance, but her plans and destination had been so indefinite she hadn't wanted to commit herself. As it was, if she hadn't seen Wade's chair, she might have been back in Georgetown by now.

Wade. She grinned at the thought of how irritated he'd be when he discovered she was spending the weekend at his family's house. That played a major role in her decision to accept the invitation, along with the fact that she didn't feel like driving more than fifty miles in what would soon be the pitch black of isolated country roads. Plus, she'd have the chance to learn more about him from his family, as well as see him again.

From the store, Coot and Millie's home was "down the road a piece," as Coot had said, and she found it easily. The house was a rambling, nineteenth-century white-frame structure with a gabled roof and black trim. The red door promised a warm welcome. Two huge blue spruces and a white picket fence sheltered the house from the graveled lane. Shasta daisies, marigolds and zinnias bordered the pillared porch that ran across the front of the house.

Apparently expecting her, Coot and Millie waved from their seat on the porch swing and came forward as Ashby climbed out of the car. "There's a garage around at the back," Millie told her, brushing aside her explanations and apologies. "We left the door open.

You don't want to leave such a nice car out here on the road."

Ashby thanked her, climbed back into the Porsche and restarted the engine. Coot joined her in the garage as she put up the black convertible top and locked her car doors. "No call to do that," he said. "This here's the country, girl."

"Force of habit," Ashby answered with a smile. She moved to the trunk and pulled out her suitcases, which Coot insisted he carry despite her objections. She gave in rather than risk offending him by mentioning his limp. They closed the garage door and joined Millie on the front porch.

"I appreciate your invitation to stay," Ashby told her. "There were no other rooms available and, as Coot said, your son is a stubborn cuss."

Coot cackled gleefully. "Don't you give up, girl."

"I don't intend to, but I insist on paying for my room."

Millie smiled but said nothing as Ashby entered the house. An intricately carved wooden banister lined a stairway to the upper floor. A set of deer antlers mounted on one wall served as a hat rack and a child's chair with an antique Victorian doll seated on it filled one corner of the spacious foyer.

"Yes, that's one of Wade's." Millie answered Ashby's unspoken question as her gaze fixed on that corner. Coot set down the suitcases as Ashby knelt to examine the chair.

"Beautiful," she breathed, giving in to the urge to set the doll aside and pick up the chair to caress the smooth wood. This one was crafted in a simpler style than the one she'd seen in the store. Y-shaped limbs still formed the straight backrest, but the boughs that served as back supports were trimmed and joined by an arched branch that gave the chair a Gothic look.

"He uses the old mortise-and-tenon style, doesn't he?" she asked as she studied the joints.

"Don't need no nails nor a speck of glue," Coot said proudly. "Fit dry rungs onto green legs and when the legs dry and tighten 'round the rungs you cain't get a better joint. Made some of the stuff myself till the rheumatiz gnarled up my fingers. Used straight pieces, though, not them fancy splints."

"But you taught Wade?"

Coot nodded. "He'd come visit as a boy and set down in my workshop and be real quiet for a spell, just a-watchin' with big eyes, then start asking the durndest questions. Got so I give him somethin' to do to shet him up."

"I still have the first stool he made," Millie said, a soft smile curving her lips. "He was ten years old and proud and shy all at the same time. It was my birthday and he'd wrapped it with a big red bow...."

"And that golldurned man of yours wanted to use it for firewood!"

Millie sighed and turned to Ashby. "It didn't go with our French Provincial furniture. Abe was..."

"A no-good, no-account..."

"A driven man." Millie's voice rose over Coot's. "No need for Ashby to listen to us squabble. Let's get her settled. It's almost time for supper." Coot still grumbled under his breath, but he picked up the suitcases and followed his daughter up the stairs. Ashby lagged behind, pausing for one more look at the perfect proportions of the child's chair before reseating the doll.

"So Wade didn't grow up here in Hickory?" she asked casually as she joined them at the top of the stairs. Too

much work went into his furniture for it to be the hobby
he said it was. Something was holding him back and she
needed to learn as much about him as she could in order to change his mind. No one could create such
beauty and not need an audience to appreciate it.

"Would 'a been better off," Coot answered. "Got
drug all over the world, instead."

"Abe was a diplomat," Millie explained, moving
across the hall and opening a door. "This will be your
room."

A pencil-post bed with a roped canopy fringed with
lace rose toward the ceiling, and a polished mahogany
highboy gleamed against one wall. A small pine table
flanked with ladder-back chairs sat in a windowed bay
that looked out over the green lawn sloping downhill
to the Potomac River.

"You may regret this," Ashby said only half jok-
ingly. "This is so beautiful, I could move in perma-
nently!"

"That's the idea." Coot cackled and winked at Millie.

Ashby's smile wavered. Wade was right, she realized. His family's hospitality had more to do with
matchmaking than with selling his furniture. Was it
wrong of her to stay when neither he nor she had any
intention of cooperating? The man was attractive, but
they mixed about as well as oil and water. But how
could she leave? She'd received the first piece of the
puzzle that was Wade Masters, and she longed for
more.

Having traveled the world as a child, he must have
chosen to settle in the only place he'd known as home,
she mused, stifling a niggling suspicion that the man
might prove as interesting as his furniture.

"These stairs—" Millie claimed her attention as she moved across the room "—lead down to the kitchen and the bath is across the hall from that. I'm afraid there's only one. It's an old house."

"No problem," Ashby assured her.

"Well, get yourself cleaned up and settled in. You'll find a sink and a mirror in the alcove on the other side of the stairway. Come on down when you're ready. Supper should be ready when you are."

Ashby opened her mouth to object, but Millie silenced her with a stern look. "Now don't insult me by refusing. If you're staying in my house, you'll eat at my table."

Ashby smiled as she nodded, then imitated Millie's sternness. "But I will pay my way."

Millie's hand fluttered dismissively. "We'll talk about that later."

After warning her that he got ornery if he had to wait too long for supper, Coot followed his daughter down the stairs. Ashby found the alcove hidden by a flowered drape she'd thought covered a window. An old marble-topped washstand bearing a china pitcher in a matching washbowl stood next to the sink. She groaned at her reflection in the mirror. As she'd feared, her curls stuck out in a halo around her head. No wonder Wade hadn't taken her seriously. She looked like a blond cherub. Or worse, a blond bimbo.

When would she see him again? Not tonight. She remembered him telling Coot to tell his mother he'd see her tomorrow. Sunday. She'd be sure to look her most professional.

For now, she wouldn't bother with the laborious process of straightening her hair. But she did refresh herself. She felt comfortable with Millie and Coot, felt comfortable in the old house. Almost, she mused, like she was home. A silly thought, but there was no need to "doody up" for dinner, as her mother would have said.

She slipped into a simply cut blue sundress and opted for a pair of thongs she'd packed in case she went swimming. She didn't, she assured herself, prefer the comfort of bare feet. Her legs were tired from her up-hill climb to Wade's farm.

The rubber-soled shoes flip-flopped on the stairs as she used her private entrance to the kitchen. The door barely budged at her light twist on the knob and she pushed harder, thinking the old wood had swollen with the day's heat. But it gave suddenly and she found herself flying down three more steps—and landing in Wade's lap.

3

"WHAT THE...?" Wade's arms automatically circled and caught Ashby before momentum carried her to the floor, but he raged inwardly. He'd come to tell his mother and grandfather to cease and desist their matchmaking efforts. Sending a woman to his home was going too damned far, and now that very same woman was in his arms!

And felt good, he had to admit. Since chance had dumped her into his lap, why not take full advantage? He pulled her closer against his chest and leaned back in the rocking chair beside the steps leading to the door of the stairway.

Their faces were close, too close, Ashby thought. Wade's mouth hovered over hers and the breath she'd lost in surprise caught in her throat as she imagined how those lips would feel against her own. Firm, warm, heavy with the promise of passion...

He looked up, away from her. Her gaze followed his to Millie, who stood by the stove across the big kitchen, and Ashby shook herself out of her reverie. What in the world was she doing sitting in Wade's lap and imagining his kiss? She tried to stand, but, to her surprise, he tightened his grip.

"Mother, you shouldn't have," Wade said, a grin tugging the corners of his lips upward as he felt Ashby squirm. If she thought to coerce him into selling his furniture by going along with his family's matchmaking, he'd make her pay. "A strawberry pie would've been enough of a dessert. Or is this an aperitif?"

He nibbled on the side of Ashby's neck and she cringed away from the tickling-yet-seductive sensation, but his large hands held her firmly in place.

"Mmm . . . smells good," he murmured, moving his lips against her silky skin. "Tastes good, too. You've outdone yourself this time, Mom. Absolutely delicious."

Ashby squirmed and wiggled, but couldn't escape his nibbling forays on her neck and throat. She finally held still, aware that her movements intensified the disturbing contact of their bodies.

"Do you mind?" she said with as much coldness as she could muster, which, she realized miserably, wasn't much. His touch warmed her from the inside out and the heat she felt in her cheeks told her she was dangerously close to blushing.

"Not at all," he mumbled, his lips now caressing the curve from her neck to her shoulder. Revenge, he decided, was very, very sweet.

"That's enough, Wade." Millie came to Ashby's aid at last, but the smile on her face contradicted the reproach in her voice. "Leave the poor girl alone."

Wade raised his head without releasing Ashby. "But isn't this why she's here?"

Coot limped into the kitchen at that moment. His wrinkled face broke into a wide grin at the sight of Ashby on Wade's lap. "Well, I'll be!"

Ashby took advantage of Wade's distraction to slip free. "No, that is not why I'm here," she said, struggling for dignity. "I'm here because there's not a hotel room to rent within fifty miles."

Wade hid his disappointment at her escape as he leaned back in his rocking chair, cocked one eyebrow skeptically and crossed his arms over his chest. "Oh?"

"It may also surprise your overly inflated ego," she continued, longing to wipe the smug smile off his face, "to learn that I'm more interested in your furniture than in you."

"Hear that, Mom?" Wade said. "She's not going along with your plans." Which was too bad; the prospect of taking advantage of her compliance and exploring the soft curves he'd held so briefly was appealing.

"What plans, dear?" Millie was all innocence as she stirred water into the pan drippings from the ham slices she'd fried, but Coot cackled.

"Pretty little thing, ain't she?" the older man said as he sat down at the kitchen table.

"That she is," Wade agreed. He offered Ashby a warm, intimate smile as an old adage occurred to him—If You Can't Beat Them, Join Them.

Ashby stared at him a moment, noticing how the warmth of his smile made the green of his eyes glow beneath his jet black hair. Confused by his switch from antagonist to apparent suitor, she turned away.

"May I set the table for you?" she asked Millie and yanked open the drawer that the older woman indicated contained silverware. Her path to the dining room took her past Wade, but she gave him a wide berth. What kind of game was he playing? she wondered, as she saw his head swivel so he could watch her each time she passed.

He'd provided most of the meal, she learned over dinner. The peas were from his garden and he'd not only cured the ham over hickory fires and seasoned it for a year in his smokehouse, he'd also raised the pig.

"Slaughtered it myself," Wade told her, making a slicing motion across his neck and watching her intently to see how she'd react to his self-sufficient lifestyle on the farm.

Ashby deliberately took another bite of ham as she returned his stare. Did he hope to ruin her appreciation of the meal by reminding her that the meat had an origin other than a tidy package in a grocery store?

"My family raised pigs and chickens," she said evenly. "We had a milk cow, too. As soon as my hands were big enough to tug on a teat, I got the daily job of milking her."

Wade's gaze dropped to her manicured fingernails and shook his head disbelievingly. He could imagine those hands stroking his body, but wrapped around a cow's teat?

Ashby turned to Millie, who gently prodded her for more information about her childhood. "We were poor," she admitted, buttering a piece of the freshly baked corn bread. "Eight kids and two adults in a house not half as large as this one. Dad worked in the coal mines when he could, but work was never steady. We raised our own food out of necessity." Her glance at Wade was pointed. After seeing this house and his farm, she doubted that he raised pigs because he had no other choice.

That information, Wade knew, confirmed his family's opinion of her as his perfect mate. Hell, it almost convinced him.... He held Ashby's gaze and toasted her with a fork laden with the creamy orange of a sweet potato dotted with black walnuts before bringing the food to his mouth.

"Plenty of mine work in my early days," Coot said, and Ashby wrenched her attention away from the gleam in Wade's green eyes and the slow progress of the fork to his lips. But she could still see him in her peripheral vision. That gleam seemed to offer both challenge and invitation. And had his lips formed a kiss before biting into his food?

"But I wasn't about to go down one of them black holes." Coot was still talking and Ashby struggled to listen as Wade's steady gaze pulled at her, its heat accelerating her pulse until her heart seemed to beat in her ears, making it hard to hear.

"Hired on with a farmer instead and done married the farmer's daughter. Made enough money to buy this house like my pappy swore he would when he helped build it as a young pup." Coot paused as he reached for the red-eye gravy and ladled it onto his ham. He offered the sauce to Wade, who shook his head without taking his eyes off Ashby.

"Blessed my lucky stars once t' oil and them land-restoration laws drove so many out of the coal business," the garrulous old man continued, warming to his subject. How could he be so oblivious to the seductive currents sizzling across the table from Wade to her? Ashby wondered, keeping her gaze on him and avoiding Wade's.

"Still had to scramble, though. Sold gas on the side and worked for a spell as sheriff, too."

"And Mom gave piano lessons," Millie added. "We didn't have a lot, but more than most." She laid her knife and fork across her empty plate. "And we *always* cleaned our plates at the reminder we were lucky to have so much to eat." She looked pointedly at the food still on Wade's and Ashby's dinner plates.

"Not even a small piece of ham, Wade?" she asked, and Ashby noticed that Wade had taken only potatoes and peas. "I would have fixed something else if I'd known you were coming."

"This is fine, Mom."

"I don't think you have to go to such an extreme—"

"My life, my choice," Wade interrupted firmly.

Why wouldn't he eat the ham? Ashby wondered as she took a bite of the succulent meat, able to eat now that his unnerving gaze was no longer fixed on her.

"Let the boy be," Coot said as Millie opened her mouth to argue. "Now as I was sayin'—" he turned back to Ashby "—we was a respectable family in these parts and Millie could've married any boy in town and she done run off with that no-good Abe Masters." Coot waved his fork at his daughter, who rolled her eyes. Wade grinned at his mother. Ashby smiled, guessing that the two were familiar with this argument.

"Apple of my eye, she was," Coot continued. "Broke her dear departed mother's heart. Oldest daughter and she climbed out a window in the middle of the night, 'stead of lettin' her parents put on a proper weddin'." He looked so outraged, Ashby had to stifle a laugh.

"You wouldn't give me permission to marry Abe," his daughter reminded him.

"He wasn't good enough for you!"

"He came from the wrong side of the tracks," Wade explained in an aside to Ashby. The last to finish with his meal, he pushed away his plate and folded his arms across his broad chest.

"Mother was a drunk and didn't know who the father was," Coot muttered.

"And he enlisted in the army, went to college on the GI Bill, joined the foreign service and provided well for me and my son," Millie said proudly.

"And didn't let you come home for eight years, never did come with you and left you a widderwoman at fifty!"

Millie shook her head and began stacking plates. "There's no arguing with you," she said, but the look she gave her father was tender. As Ashby helped clear the table, she was surprised to see Wade carrying dishes, too. Coot pulled out a pipe and began to fill it from a pouch in his breast pocket.

"Not in the house," Millie said.

"My house," Coot grumbled.

"You agreed," she reminded him sweetly. "Ten years ago, when I moved home," Coot muttered but left the table, and Ashby heard the front door slam as she followed Wade and his mother to the kitchen.

"Sometimes I don't know why I came back," Millie said with a shake of her head. She wrapped leftovers and put them in the refrigerator, while Wade rinsed plates and filled the dishwasher. Watching, Ashby saw that the routine was an established one and sat down at the kitchen table rather than get in the way.

"Because you prefer Hickory to Paris or Washington," Wade answered, his glance sweeping over to Ashby.

Millie paused to gaze out the window over the green slope of the backyard. "And I prefer country ham, corn bread and red-eye gravy to sole meunière," she added softly, then turned to Ashby. "How about you? What brings you back to West Virginia?"

Not *that* question. Ashby suddenly found the old china salt-and-pepper shakers on the kitchen table of utmost interest. But she could still see Wade in her peripheral vision. As he turned away from the dishwasher to face her, she sensed his tension.

"Well..." A part of her wanted to admit she didn't know why she was there. "Um..." Another part wanted to provide the glib excuse of her craft show. Absently fiddling with the salt-and-pepper shakers, she fell completely silent, astounded to realize that yet a third part of her wanted to laugh, to confess she was turning thirty-five and losing her mind!

"She owns an art gallery—" Wade broke the silence "—and wants to show the city folks how artistic the poor folks are." He paused. "And make a few bucks for herself, of course. She's a businesswoman." He made the term sound like an epithet, angry that she'd been able to ignore him and listen to Coot at the dinner table when he couldn't take his eyes off her.

"Wade Masters!" Millie's voice was sharp with rebuke, while Ashby sputtered and spilled the salt and pepper. "You sound just like your father." She shook her head sadly. "Abe had a big heart but felt he had to hide it behind a wall of cynicism. Wade seems to have inherited that trait."

"A faulty heart, not a big one," her son corrected. Millie opened her mouth to speak, but Wade cut her off. "Where are you hiding those strawberries I picked for you? Please, don't tell me you used them all for jam."

He crossed the room and opened the refrigerator, while Ashby surreptitiously swept the scattered grains of salt and pepper into her hand and into her pocket. What had Wade meant by a faulty heart? she wondered. He was so big, so strong, she couldn't imagine him with a weak or faulty anything.

"Aha! I knew it." Wade pulled out a pie piled high with strawberries so huge and ripely red that Ashby's mouth watered.

He set the pie on the kitchen table as Coot rejoined them and the subject changed to a choice of coffee or sassafras tea. Wade scowled, while Coot beamed with approval when she chose the latter.

Millie made whipped cream and they sat at the kitchen table to eat the strawberry pie. "Are you going to the fair in Clairmont tomorrow?" Millie asked Ashby.

Ashby nodded as she swallowed a strawberry. "I hope to find more cooperative craftspeople than your son."

Wade grinned at her barbed comment, then winced as his mother invited her to their family picnic on the fairgrounds. His aunts, uncles and cousins would be in attendance and, he knew, willing accomplices in the matchmaking scheme.

He paused in the act of raising a huge, sugar-glazed strawberry to his lips. "Let's get something straight, right now," he said, setting the strawberry back on his plate with a show of extreme patience. The fact that Ashby was the first woman his family had thrown at him that attracted him failed to ease his irritation at their matchmaking. He'd made his peace with the direction his life had taken; he wanted no more upheavals.

"This woman—" he pointed his fork at Ashby "—may have been born here, but she's a city woman now. Quit encouraging her to stay in hopes that I'm going to fall head over heels in love with her and start a family. I'm too old. And she's too young. If she's a day over thirty to my thirty-nine, I'll eat my hat." He speared another strawberry. "And she's too short."

Ashby listened to Wade dismiss her in silence, but she couldn't let him get away with a slur on her height. She turned to Millie. "Where's his hat?"

Coot cackled and jumped up from the table, then returned with a battered baseball cap emblazoned with the insignia of the Chicago White Sox. Ashby passed Wade the whipped cream as Coot handed him the hat. "This might improve the flavor."

"I don't eat cream." Wade ignored the hat as he stared at Ashby. "How old are you?"

"I'll be thirty-five in August."

"Bull!"

"Would you like to see my driver's license?"

"Yes!"

Ashby dashed up the stairs to her bedroom. When she returned, she handed the plastic card to Wade with a flourish, then stood over him as he studied it.

"'Ashby Carol White,'" he read aloud, "'five foot two, ninety-eight pounds,'" he raised his eyes from the card to carefully examine her small stature and slender curves.

"The birth date," she reminded him, resisting the urge to shift from one foot to the other and betray her discomfort.

"Oh, yes." He returned to his study of the card. He'd already performed the mental calculations necessary to figure that she wasn't lying about her age. But he played for time, seeking a means to gain the advantage in their sparring. "'Blue eyes, blond hair. Birth date, August sixteenth,'" he finished, tossing the plastic card onto the table. He gripped her waist with his hands and pulled her closer to stand between his knees. "What would you like for your birthday?"

The clatter of forks dropping onto plates and chairs scraping against the linoleum floor announced Coot and Millie's hasty departure. Ashby steadily returned Wade's gaze.

"Your furniture." She made no move to free herself. Her strength, she'd already learned, was no match for his.

"Forget it." He released her quickly, but Ashby decided to give him a dose of his own medicine and twined her arms around his neck. Opening her eyes wide, she batted her eyelashes at him.

"Just one piece? Maybe a child's chair like your mother's?" She curled her fingers into the thick hair that brushed the back of his neck and pressed closer. A mistake, she realized instantly, as her heartbeat leaped at the feel of his hard chest beneath her breasts and at the answering flare of desire she saw in his eyes.

His hands came up to stroke her back in sensual circles. "Just how far are you willing to go to get that chair?"

"Not that far." She pulled back quickly. He watched her move around the table and out of reach, his eyes heavy lidded.

She sat down and dug into her strawberry pie, although she no longer had any appetite for it. "Aren't you going to eat your hat?"

"You have whipped cream—" he pointed to the right corner of his mouth "—here." Ashby licked the spot with a quick flick of her tongue, an action he watched with great interest.

"Since you are of suitable age," he drawled huskily, "I'd rather spread whipped cream all over your body

and lick it clean." What the hell, he swore silently.
Maybe his family had a point. However content he was
on the farm, he did occasionally miss feminine com-
panionship. And maybe there was truth in that old adage he'd remembered earlier—If You Can't Beat Them,
Join Them.

This woman was not only physically attractive, she
was intelligent and caring. She was not a pushover.
And nothing inspired him like a challenge. He grinned,
feeling the old heady exhilaration begin to course
through his veins. He'd once thrived on speculation, on
calculated risk. And he'd excelled at it—until his body
could no longer keep up with his mind.

The pursuit of this tiny blonde couldn't endanger the
health of his heart, he assured himself. And he'd please
his family by appearing to surrender to their matchmaking. Plus, the differences between Ashby and him
were too great for the relationship to develop into a
threat to his chosen life-style. When she left, as she in-
evitably would, he could appear brokenhearted and his
family would stop trying to mate him with every available woman under fifty.

He grinned, pleased with his plan, and watched
Ashby swallow a strawberry with great care, as if afraid
she might choke.

"I thought—" Ashby paused to swallow again, aware
that her voice had come out no stronger than a squeak
"—you didn't like whipped cream."

"It depends on what it's served with." His gaze wandered over her so slowly and sensually that she had to
repress a shiver.

"But you said I'm not your type." Ashby's pleasure
that her voice had strengthened was diluted with the
knowledge that she felt way out of her depth.

"You're not, any more than I'm yours. But we're not talking marriage here, are we?" Mesmerized by those green eyes and unable to think of a smart answer, Ashby stared at him.

"No, we're not," he decided for her. "But perhaps a summer romance?"

Ashby shook herself out of her trance as she realized he was suggesting they have an affair. "I don't, for your information, jump into bed with every man I meet."

Wade grinned. "I didn't think you did." He paused, needing a moment to digest a surprising flash of relief that his guess was right. "I can see you in your city duds." He squinted at her, imagining the scene. "All sophisticated and elegant, turning those big blue eyes into ice cubes and freezing a man in his tracks."

"But you think I would jump into bed with you?" Ashby did her best to sound scornful.

Wade grinned. "Lady, I felt you quiver when I touched you."

Unable to deny the truth of his words, Ashby dropped her gaze to the strawberries on her plate. She started nervously when she heard him rise. "Think about it," he said as he left. "I'll see you at the fair tomorrow."

She wouldn't even consider such an outrageous, cold-blooded proposition, she told herself. Yet, when she joined Coot and Millie on the front porch, she couldn't rid her mind of it. And once she went to bed, there was nothing to stop the dizzying circles spinning in her brain.

"Your biological clock is running, sweetie," she remembered her sister and best friend, Sue, telling her when she'd admitted to the strange restlessness gripping her at the approach of her birthday. "You've made a success of your gallery and now you want a family. At your age, you don't have much time left. The baby would be easy enough to have, but you want a man who'll stay around and be a husband and father."

And that man would not be Wade Masters. She couldn't even persuade him to sell her his furniture!

"You're going back to West Virginia," Sue had insisted, "because no matter how much you think you hated your childhood, you had family there. And that's what you're looking for now."

"Ridiculous," Ashby muttered aloud and rolled over to stare up at the canopy over her bed. But her sister's arguments continued to ring in her head.

"Remember Ron Jenkins?" Sue had reminded her of her high-school sweetheart. "You were heartbroken when he got tired of waiting for you to finish college and married Kitty Lou. How many other men looked elsewhere when you couldn't squeeze in time for them because you were working two jobs to save money for your gallery? And once you got it, you were working eighteen-hour days, seven days a week. And don't try to argue. I know because you rarely had time for me, either!"

As usual, her older sister was right. Ashby had meant to postpone marriage, not rule it out. And, while she was at it, she may as well admit that Wade Masters, the man, interested her as much as Wade Masters, the furniture maker. And interested her more than any of the men she was currently seeing on her typically casual basis. She flopped over onto her side.

But Wade had made it clear he wasn't offering marriage, and he was too cynical, rude and arrogant for her. Although, a little voice in her head reminded her, he seemed very close with his mother and grandfather. The man could be gentle, kind, even loving.

Great. A relationship with a man like that would be like riding an emotional seesaw. She would not become involved with Wade Masters. She was too vulnerable. What she wanted was a husband and a family, and she'd tell him that. She smiled as she thought of his reaction. He would run from her, as Coot had put it, "like a scairt jackrabbit."

4

WADE LEANED AGAINST the side of his truck parked beneath the leafy canopy of an ancient oak and stared down the road that curved along the banks of the Potomac River to the fairgrounds. Fiddling with a small branch he'd found beneath the tree, he alternately peeled off its dried bark and lifted it in greeting as acquaintances pulled into the dusty parking lot.

He tensed when he recognized the polished black gleam of Coot's vintage 1937 Ford truck toiling up the road. One look at Ashby, he figured, and he'd know the answer to his question. He hoped she'd say yes, but he doubted that she would. His proposition had lacked finesse, to put it mildly. He'd forgotten how to woo a woman.

He tightened his grip on the stick in his hands as Coot parked the old Ford fifty feet away. Rather than move to join them, Wade remained where he was as he watched Ashby follow his mother out the passenger side of the truck.

No, he decided, the answer was a definite no. The crack of snapping wood told him he'd broken the stick, and he tossed the pieces aside without taking his eyes off the small blonde.

Not a curl remained on her head. Her short hair was swept back from her face in a sleek style that made her look closer to her thirty-five years. And her clothes . . . Not for her a simple shirtdress like his mother's or a pair of blue jeans or shorts like other younger women. No, she wore a flared, finely-spun cotton skirt with tiny white flowers dotted on a black background. Her white French-cut T-shirt was casual, but the wide red belt and matching wedge-heeled soft leather shoes screamed of the sophistication that attracted him yet warned him that if he won her, he'd never keep her.

Forewarned was forearmed. He had no illusions that she'd fall in love with him. But fate had crossed their paths, his family had thrown them together, and he was going to enjoy the pursuit. No more, no less.

As he pushed himself away from the truck, he saw her reach back into the cab for her purse. She flipped the red strap of the shoulder bag over her head and crossed it between her breasts. Its positioning, Wade knew from his city living, served to keep her hands free and also avoided purse snatching.

She looked up at his approach. "You don't have to do that," he said. "This is Clairmont, not Georgetown. No one is going to grab your pocketbook." Red nail polish had replaced the pink of the previous day, and equally red hoop earrings completed her ensemble.

She shrugged as she slipped sunglasses onto her nose without meeting his gaze. "I'm comfortable with it this way." She turned toward Coot and Millie. "Ready?"

Wade's grin of greeting widened as he watched his relatives thwart Ashby's effort to avoid him. They nodded to her, smiled at him, then stepped closer together and moved ahead, leaving her no choice but to walk with him.

"No, eh?" he asked, careful to match his pace with hers.

"No, what?" She stared straight ahead.

"No, you're not going to indulge in a country romance with me."

She kept walking, still not looking at him. "As I told you last night, I'm not interested in a meaningless affair in the city or the country."

"Who said it had to be meaningless?"

Her step faltered. "A country romance?" she snapped as she faced him. "You put fancy words on nothing but a sexual proposition. And *that* is meaningless!"

"We wouldn't spend all our time in bed." Wade adopted a reasonable, if tongue-in-cheek tone. "Once we got all this sexual tension out of the way, maybe we could have a conversation rather than argue all the time."

Ashby shook her head, started to run her fingers through her hair, then remembered how hard she'd worked to straighten it. "The answer is no." She resumed walking toward the fairgrounds. "Accept that and we can stop arguing."

"Okay." Wade kept pace beside her and she glanced at him, suspicious of, she told herself, not disappointed in, his ready acceptance of her refusal.

He grinned, but kept his thoughts to himself. He didn't blame her for rejecting his blunt proposal. He'd have to hone his rusty courting skills and try a different tack. That was all. Once he'd set a goal for himself, he wasn't one to give up.

He whistled cheerfully as they reached the noise and confusion of the fairgrounds. The Ferris wheel spun off to their left, accompanied by the shrieks of children and the tinkling harmony of the nearby merry-go-round. The aromas of popcorn, pizza and fried onions competed for his appetite, but he chose to stop by a vendor selling candy apples.

"A peace offering?" he asked Ashby, indicating the red-glazed fruit.

Ashby paused reluctantly, not wanting to lose sight of Coot and Millie, who continued on ahead. But neither did she want to miss an opportunity to establish a friendship with Wade and improve her chances of persuading him to sell his furniture.

"I don't think I've had one since I was little," she murmured, as she remembered the fairs of her childhood. She'd clutched the pitiful allowance her parents could afford in her grubby little hand as she'd agonized over what she wanted more. A candy apple or cotton candy? A ride on the swings or the merry-go-round? Never had lessons in addition and subtraction been so quickly learned.

"I'd love an apple," she said, silently promising herself all the rides and candy that struck her fancy today.

Wade bought two and handed her one. She brought it to her lips, then hesitated, eyeing it thoughtfully. "I don't know if an apple is a suitable token of peace. Remember what happened to Adam and Eve?"

Wade chuckled and bit into the apple, his teeth white against the red candy coating. "But you already said no and I accepted your answer," he reminded her when he'd swallowed. "Or is the 'no' really a 'maybe'?"

Ashby raised an eyebrow in disdain, then bit into the apple decisively. She didn't want him to guess how tempting she'd found his proposition. "What I'm really looking for," she said, deciding to play what she thought of as her ace in the hole, "is a husband and family." Smiling, she waited for him to turn tail and run.

He didn't. He eyed her speculatively as he finished his apple. "You're not married to your gallery?"

He was, Ashby fumed, taking the offensive rather than retreating. She busied herself with her own apple and glanced around for Coot and Millie. The crowd had swallowed them.

"I was," she admitted, forcing herself to meet his expectant gaze. She found it discomfiting that he'd so quickly recognized her dedication to her gallery. Was her sister right in guessing that the other men in her life saw it, too? Or was this man more perceptive than most?

"But you're not anymore?" Wade pressed. Rather than feeling intimidated by her assertion that she was husband hunting, he was intrigued.

"My gallery is a success and I've found a manager I trust. I didn't have time to devote to a family before, but I do now."

"Any likely candidates in mind?"

The gleam in Wade's eyes made her suspect that he wasn't taking her marital intentions any more seriously than he did her interest in his furniture.

"Not you, that's for sure." She'd meant to speak lightly, but she could hear the edge in her voice betraying her lie.

He again wore jeans, a tad less faded than the ones he'd worn yesterday, but they were just as snug fitting and possibly rode even lower on his hips. The mint color of his short-sleeved shirt emphasized the darkness of his sun-bronzed skin and the knit fabric hugged the curves of sinew and muscle. Dark curls peeked out of the open neck.

A perfect specimen to father a child . . . *But personality,* she informed her hormones, *is as important in a husband as physical attributes, so cool it!*

Wade grinned. "Oh, but you haven't gotten to know me yet," he said. "And at your age, you shouldn't rule out any possibilities. Statistically, it's more likely that you'll be hit by a car than marry."

He was, Ashby decided as she glared at him, impervious to insult. But she couldn't dispute his depressing statistics; she'd read of similar studies. Refusing to respond, she snatched napkins from the vendor, wiped her mouth and hands, then tossed apple and paper into a trash can.

Wade followed suit, but she didn't wait for him. He caught up with her as she roamed through the craft displays. She ignored him as she fingered quilts, crocheted doilies and hand-embroidered pillowcases, admired pinecone and dried-flower wreaths, hand-tooled leather belts and wood carvings.

All were attractive, Ashby thought, but she wanted nothing short of exceptional for her gallery. Would she have been so picky if she hadn't seen Wade's furniture? Everything else seemed mundane in comparison.

She wished he'd grow bored with her slow perusals and wander off on his own, but instead he made small talk with the craftspeople. Most of whom, she realized as she eavesdropped, were local and known to him already. The women, regardless of age, seemed especially attentive.

"Nothing good enough?" he asked, as they passed an empty space between booths.

"It's all very nice, but I'm looking for something unique." She cast him a sidelong glance. "Like your furniture."

"If I accept no for an answer, why can't you?"

Ashby halted, glad to seize the opportunity to try to persuade him again. "Because it would be such a waste of your talent to let it go unrecognized."

He grinned, but his voice was low and husky, full of sensual promise. "And it would be a shame to waste the chemistry between us by letting it go unfulfilled."

Ashby blinked as she felt the leap of her heart agree with him. But she forced herself to shake her head with an aggravated air and move to the next booth before Wade could sense the lie.

Her hopes of finding anything for her gallery were sinking fast, but she stuck to her search. The fair was a small one in honor of Independence Day, its main attraction being the carnival with its rides and games. The craft booths, Ashby guessed, had been added in recent years to attract tourists.

"You'd have better luck at the county fairs at the end of the summer," Wade said, as if reading her thoughts.

"Too late." Ashby shook her head. "I want to have everything and be back in Georgetown by September so I can open the exhibit in the fall."

"And whatever Ashby wants, Ashby gets?"

Her chin lifted. "I've worked for everything I have."

Looking down at her, Wade believed her. Her story of growing up poor hadn't been concocted to impress him or his family. The chains of poverty were strong, he knew, and suddenly he wanted to know how she'd broken them.

"Look at that!" Ashby's face lit up with excitement and she made a beeline for a booth farther down the row. Wade followed her slowly, wondering just who the real Ashby White was. Neither the polished sophisticate nor the little gamin with curly blond hair and big blue eyes, he suspected. Someone in-between. Someone very strong. And fascinating.

"Hello, Anna." He murmured his greeting to his cousin to avoid interrupting Ashby's praise of her quilt. Two years older than he, Anna had been his best friend and playmate when he'd visited Hickory as a child. Anna had married instead of pursuing her dream of attending art school and they'd drifted apart until he'd returned to live on Coot's farm.

A tall, slim woman with long brown hair tied back at the nape of her neck, his cousin glanced at him uncertainly. Wade guessed she didn't know what to make of the elegant blonde exclaiming over her talent.

"The workmanship is excellent," Ashby was saying as she examined the tiny stitches. "And the design. It's a painting in fabric. You have a real eye for color."

Instead of depicting a Colonial theme like the wedding knot, the shapes and colors pictured a landscape. Deep shades of green defined tree-clad mountains in the distance, while brighter hues in the foreground gave the impression of a grassy meadow dotted with wildflowers. Fluffy white clouds floated in a light blue sky and narrow, arched strips of dark fabric captured the grace of the outstretched wings of flying birds.

"This is like your furniture." Ashby turned to Wade excitedly. "Traditional methods used to create a more modern effect." And like Wade's furniture, Ashby silently vowed, she *had* to have the quilt. The folk-art exhibit was no longer a half-baked idea in her mind, but a set goal, perfect for the Thanksgiving and Christmas seasons when attention turned toward home and family.

She launched into her sales pitch, explaining the advantages of showing in her gallery, the higher price the quilt could command despite the added expense of her own commission and the expanded scope of the Georgetown market.

Wade saw the growing confusion on Anna's face. Pride mixed with skepticism as she listened to Ashby's rush of words. He stepped forward slightly and caught his cousin's eye, then nodded to assure her that Ashby was indeed who and what she said she was.

Ashby noticed the exchange and glanced at Wade gratefully. In her enthusiasm, she'd been pushing too hard and too fast. The woman probably made quilts as a hobby to supplement her family's income. She wasn't an artist who dreamed of pursuing a career with her talent.

"You know one another?" Ashby asked, realizing that Wade's presence by her side could prove to be more than an annoying distraction. She should have remembered a native West Virginian's suspicion of outsiders. She needed to temper her direct approach and win their trust.

"We're kissin' cousins," Anna volunteered. "Played house when we was small and taught one another to kiss when we was teenagers." She grinned at Wade.

I bet he caught on fast, Ashby thought, but clamped her lips together before she spoke aloud. She didn't dare look at Wade for fear she'd be unable to keep herself from staring at his lips and wondering what his kiss would be like.

"Devastated my ego when she got the giggles," Wade said mournfully. "I still haven't recovered."

"Ha!" Ashby's laugh of disbelief escaped her at the same time as Anna's, seeming to soften the older woman's reserve.

"You really want to show my quilt in your gallery?" she asked shyly.

Ashby nodded. "It would show especially well on a bed with a headboard made by your cousin." She turned to Wade.

"Oh, no." He backed up a step. "Don't involve me in this. That quilt can sell on its own." The disappointment that crossed Anna's face made him scowl at Ashby.

"It's not a package deal," he assured his cousin and turned pointedly back to Ashby. "But that was a nice try."

"No, I'm interested in your quilts regardless of how blindly stubborn Wade is," Ashby told Anna, realizing he was not a man to be manipulated. "I'm sure I can double these prices, but the exhibit won't open until the fall. Could you hold these or build another inventory?"

"I'll have to talk to my husband, John," Anna said. "He keeps saying I should charge more, what with all the time it takes to make the durn things. But people hereabouts cain't pay much, although we're starting to get more tourists."

Ashby delved into her purse. "This is my card and a copy of my standard contract." John, Ashby was certain, wouldn't be impressed with promises. "I'll give you a few days to go over the terms with your husband, and then call, if you'll give me your name and number. We can arrange a time for the three of us to discuss it." She pulled a pen and notebook from her purse and handed them to Anna.

"Quite the efficient businesswoman," Wade said, as Anna scribbled her name and address in the notebook.

"I'm good at what I do." Ashby lifted her chin and steeled herself for an insult.

"I can tell."

Ashby blinked at the unexpected praise, then turned away to hide a warm flush of pleasure. She studied Anna's photo album of quilts. Some were like abstract paintings, a kaleidoscope of colors, while others depicted wildlife and natural scenes like the one Ashby had first admired.

Many of the quilts pictured in the photo album bore blue ribbons won at county fairs. "We can get you money instead of ribbons," she promised, as Anna handed her the notebook and she tucked it back into her purse. "And if you'll draw up some designs, I'll sell on consignment, too."

"Marry that girl," Anna advised Wade as they parted, "and keep her in the family!"

"But then she'd move to the farm and who would sell your quilts for those highfalutin prices?" Wade shot back, so accustomed to his relatives' gibes about marriage, he didn't feel in the least embarrassed by the remark, but Ashby sputtered with shock.

"Coot and my mother aren't the only matchmakers in my family," he said, taking her by the arm and drawing her away from Anna's booth. "I've got a whole army of aunts, uncles and cousins conspiring to marry me off. You'll meet them at the picnic today. Consider yourself warned."

They skipped over the remaining nondescript booths and headed for the shade of a tree beside the river. Ashby knelt down on a soft spot of grass and Wade stretched out on his back beside her. Her mind raced with questions. First and foremost, she wanted to know what he had against marriage, but she wouldn't let herself ask that question. Too personal. Instead, she fixed her mind on his joking reference to her moving to his farm.

"You don't think you'd ever live in a city again?" she asked casually.

"No." His face darkened and he glanced away from her. "How do you know I lived in a city?" Although he made no discernible movement, Ashby sensed him tense.

"Your father was a diplomat. You've probably lived in cities all over the world. You probably got tired of moving around when you were a child."

"Yeah, I guess you could say that." His hands linked behind his head, he gazed up at the white frame schoolhouse topped by a huge bell tower on the hill overlooking the fairgrounds.

Ashby gritted her teeth and counted to ten. Prying secrets out of this man was not an easy task. "You know your furniture would be very popular. Why won't you sell?"

He sighed as he pulled his gaze from the schoolhouse and turned back to her. "You don't give up, do you?"

"Coot told me you were a stubborn cuss. Guess it takes one to know one," she agreed with a grin.

"You don't believe that people can be content to live without ambition?"

Ashby studied him for a moment, then shook her head. "Some people, maybe, but not you. You're too strong-minded. I can't believe you're content to spend the rest of your life on a farm."

He rolled over on his side and propped himself up on one elbow to bring his face level with hers. "Believe it." His gaze bored into hers, deadly serious. "You're right about me in one respect. I used to be ambitious but I gave it up four years ago. I don't intend to go back. Ever. For anything... or anyone."

Ashby read the warning in his green eyes: No Trespassing. Questions crowded to the tip of her tongue but died stillborn. Asking them now would only antagonize him. Retreat was the better part of valor at this point, she decided.

Apparently satisfied with her silence, Wade again leaned back against the grass. His gaze returned to the schoolhouse on top of the hill and he spoke in a soft voice.

"I wanted to live here and go to that school more than anything when I was a kid. And take the bus instead of a limousine, or walk like my parents had." He sighed. "I envied Anna and my other friends and they envied me. I've been back for four years and they still ask me why I'm here."

"And what do you answer?" Only half of her mind was on her question. The other half was busy subtracting the two years he'd said he'd been without a woman.

"Same reason they're here. I love it."

"You don't think they'd leave if they had the chance?" She found it hard to believe that anyone would choose to live in what was, to her, an economically and culturally deprived area.

Wade turned his head to look up at her. "They think they would, but if they really wanted to, they'd find a way. You did. How?"

He had, Ashby realized, turned the tables on her, deftly switching the subject to her past. But she couldn't pry into his life without revealing her own. She leaned back against the trunk of the tree behind her and stretched out her legs while she thought about what to say. The flutter of the breeze through the leaves overhead and the rippling of the river nearby created a peaceful atmosphere that seemed to encourage the sharing of secrets.

"I went to a school smaller than that," she said, raising her gaze to the schoolhouse. "And I studied . . . studied hard. My parents believed the only way their children could better themselves was through education. I won a scholarship to the University of West Virginia and majored in art. I have a little talent, but mostly I appreciated beautiful things and wanted some for myself."

She paused to consider Wade's reaction, expecting him to belittle her efforts. But he regarded her steadily, then surprised her by adjusting his position so he could lie with his head in her lap.

"And then what?" he asked, as if his action were the most natural thing in the world.

Ashby swallowed and dug her hands into the grass on each side of her to fight the urge to sink her hands into his thick hair. "Then I got a fellowship to Georgetown University and earned my master's degree," she continued, agonizingly aware of the warmth of his head in her lap. The light breeze coming off the river ruffled through his hair. She stared at the glossy black strands fluttering across his high forehead and her willpower crumbled.

Hesitantly, she reached out one hand and lightly brushed back the silky hair. His eyes closed and she grew bolder as she talked, sinking her fingers into the thick mass, lifting it and letting its satiny smoothness slide through her fingers.

"I worked as a curator at the Smithsonian on weekdays and as a clerk at a private art gallery in the evenings and weekends to make enough money to buy a town house. I converted the lower floor into a gallery five years ago, then I worked even harder." She laughed softly at herself, realizing she was quoting her sister. "And here I am!"

"You never married?" Wade could barely hear her words through the haze of pleasure created by her light touch across his forehead and through his hair.

"No." She uncurled her fingers from his hair and dropped her hand back to her side at the thought. What was she doing, falling under his spell when she was in the market for a husband rather than a lover? She needed to get her folk-art exhibit together and hightail it back to Georgetown. "What about you?" she asked nonetheless, unable to repress her curiosity.

He opened his eyes and nodded. "I was divorced two years ago."

The two years he'd been alone, Ashby figured. So his wife had come to Hickory with him, then left. "Children?" she asked.

"We never got around to them. Guess it was for the best. We were workaholics, too." Wade didn't want to talk about Kay. He stood and offered Ashby his hand to help her up. "Let's go find Mom and Coot. I'm starving, and I'm sure the picnic is ready."

Ashby took his hand and rose reluctantly. She wanted to know so much more. No, she corrected herself, she *needed* to know more. Where he'd been, what type of job he'd had, why he'd turned his back on his ambition, what had brought him back to Hickory, why his wife had left him. She had to put the puzzle of Wade Masters together, sign him to a contract for his furniture, then get on with her search for a husband.

As he led her back toward the carnival, the grip of his hand distracted her from her mission. She had the unsettling feeling that keeping her interest professional rather than personal was going to be a difficult task.

5

"CATCH OF GRANT COUNTY done got caught!" Coot called over the din of the nearby carnival as Wade and Ashby approached a line of picnic tables on the edge of the fairgrounds. Covered with red-and-white checked vinyl cloths, the tables were laden with dishes of every description and surrounded by people of all ages.

Wade tightened his grip on Ashby's hand and steered her away from his grandfather and toward his mother. Millie turned from a conversation with another woman. "Don't mind Coot," she told Ashby. "He loves to tease Wade."

"The catch of Grant County?" Ashby repeated with an amused glance at Wade.

"According to my family," Wade agreed. He glanced around the crowded line of tables, looking to see which of his numerous relatives had unattached females in tow. He saw at least three, none of them as attractive as Ashby. He released her hand and slid an arm around her shoulders to signal that he wasn't available. Several of his male cousins raised their hands in greeting, then touched thumb and forefinger together to sign approval of the petite blonde.

"The rejoicing that went on when Kay left and word got around that she wouldn't be comin' back was positively shameful," Coot said as he joined them, his cackle anything but disapproving. "We et like kings for more'n a week, what with all the dishes the local ladies done brought for poor, lonely Wade."

Kay must have been Wade's wife. Ashby glanced at Wade and saw his expression harden and close.

"I think I'll check out the game," he said curtly, glancing toward a group of men tossing horseshoes. Just to make sure the would-be matchmakers got the picture, he dropped a kiss on Ashby's head before he stalked away. For the first time, he resented Coot's teasing and the lack of privacy in small-town living. The last thing he wanted from Ashby was pity, but neither did he like the idea of her picturing him as the local Casanova.

"Have a seat," Millie said to Ashby, moving over and patting the space on the bench beside her, "and I'll make introductions."

Ashby did as she was told, although a part of her mind lingered on Wade. Was he still in love with his wife? Had her leaving hurt him so deeply that he wouldn't let another woman close to his emotions?

The man was an expert at confusing her, she fumed, but Millie's introductions demanded her full attention and she filed thoughts of Wade away for future reference. The people crowding about the tables laughed with her good-naturedly as she struggled to remember their names and relationships.

Everyone was, in some way, related to Coot, who strutted from table to table with his thumbs hooked under the straps of his bib overalls, his thin chest puffed up with the proud air of a patriarch. Not all were local residents, but it appeared that those who had moved away frequently returned to Hickory.

The family gathering, the smell of meats broiling on grills and the clang of successful horseshoe throws stirred Ashby's memories of summer Sunday afternoons spent as a child with her relatives. She had gained much since she'd left home, but had she lost something, too?

If her parents had lived, would she have visited Weathersfield? Her sister Sue kept in contact with their relatives still living there and informed her of their lives, loves and reproductions, but Ashby had long since stopped trying to keep track and figured they'd forgotten her, too. She felt a strange pang at the thought, but told herself it was just as well. She had no intention of returning to Weathersfield. She'd put that part of her life behind her.

"I'm going to gain about a million pounds," she said when Millie interrupted her musing by suggesting she eat. "I don't think I've ever seen this much food in one place!"

Barbecued ribs and chicken, country ham, roast turkey, home-baked beans, potato and macaroni salads, coleslaw, jelled and fruit salads, biscuits and corn bread filled the tables. She tried a little of everything despite the stab of hurt she felt when she noticed the game of horseshoes end and Wade sit at another table.

A table of men, she noted. The separation of the sexes was alive and well in West Virginia. What would people do if she rose and integrated that table? Assume she was chasing after Wade, she decided, and remained firmly in place. Wade Masters apparently had enough women after him and she wasn't about to join the line.

"Care for some applejack, ladies?" As if summoned by her thoughts, Wade's voice spoke behind her. She looked up to see him holding a gallon jug of amber liquid.

"You keep that likker away from my young 'uns," the woman opposite Ashby told him. "They're wild enough as it is."

Dessie was her name, Ashby remembered after a moment of concentrated effort. Millie's youngest sister, she still had two teenage boys at home and an older four with families of their own. Several of her sons had stopped by their table and treated her with a respect totally out of proportion to her small size.

"I solemnly swear never to lead your boys astray," Wade assured his aunt, "but this little lady here—" he laid a hand on Ashby's shoulder "—is well over twenty-one. And I think she'll need some loosening up before the band starts."

"You just make sure dancing's all that's on your mind," Dessie scolded.

Ashby flushed. The warm weight of Wade's large hand made her think of other forms of touching.

"So, what do you say, my lady?" Wade asked her. He didn't, Ashby noticed, respond to his aunt's remark. "Can I interest you in some applejack, peanuts and foot-stompin' music? Or would that be beneath your city sophistication?"

Stung by his implication that she would hold herself above the people who had so warmly welcomed her into their midst, Ashby stood. She lifted her chin and met the challenge in Wade's eyes.

"How could I refuse an invitation so gallantly put?" she retorted, irritated at the return of Wade's cynical guard. Was it because of Coot's mention of Kay?

The women behind her laughed and one—Ashby wasn't sure which—said, "That's right, dearie, you put that boy in his place!"

Wade ignored the comment, but Ashby turned her head to wink at the women. "No problem," she assured them.

Wade's eyes glittered with amusement when she swung her gaze back to him. "After you, *madame*." With a flourish he indicated that she precede him. "I'll walk a respectful three paces behind, laden like a pack-horse." In addition to the jug of applejack, he carried a blanket over his arm and the promised bag of peanuts.

"As you should," Ashby agreed, and she moved away from the table.

"There is one problem, my lady," Wade told her moments later and she turned. "As your most loyal servant, I must respectfully inform you that you're going in the wrong direction."

Ashby rolled her eyes. "Do lead the way, then, most humble of servants."

"Humble?" Wade grinned as he drew abreast of her. "Now that's an adjective I've never heard applied to me."

"Really? I can't imagine why." They laughed as they walked together in the direction Wade indicated. Ashby felt as sunny as the day, pleased that their banter seemed to have restored their earlier rapport.

When they reached a grassy meadow, Wade chose a spot off to the side of a small bandstand. They'd still be able to see the musicians, but they were hidden from the rest of the gathering audience by a cluster of small bushes that encroached onto the field from the woods behind them.

After Wade had spread the blanket, he unscrewed the lid of the bottle of applejack, took a swig and offered it to her. Ashby eyed it doubtfully.

"Pretty potent stuff, isn't it?"

"Don't tell me you never tried it as a kid?"

She shook her head. "My parents never drank and if any of us had dared, we knew we'd have been in for a licking if we got caught."

"Spare the rod, spoil the child?"

"They were strict but fair. And they loved us." Ashby felt defensive. She didn't like the faint disapproval she read on Wade's face. "You don't think a child should be disciplined?"

"Disciplined, yes, whipped, no." Wade shrugged away the subject. "A most important part of your West Virginia upbringing is lacking. I insist you rectify the situation at once." He held the gallon jar out to her.

Ashby would have preferred to continue the discussion of child raising. Apparently Wade had some firm opinions on the subject. She liked that in a man. He also hadn't backed off after her announcement that she had marriage in mind. Maybe, just maybe, a future with him wasn't as unlikely as she'd thought.

He pushed the jug of applejack into her hands, forcing her to take it. She glanced around their blanket. "You forgot cups."

"No, I didn't. Applejack is supposed to be drunk straight from the jug. Tastes better."

"I'll spill it all over my chin and down my shirt."

Wade's eyes gleamed wickedly. "Then I'll lick it up for you."

About to take a sip, Ashby set the jug down abruptly. Wade laughed. "Chicken?" he taunted. "Maybe that's why city people have fancy glasses for their wines and liqueurs. They're not coordinated enough to drink from the bottle!"

Ashby stuck her tongue out at him, then used both hands to lift the jug to her lips. As she sipped, Wade tilted the bottle higher and she gulped more of the home brew than she intended. Her eyes watering and her throat burning from the tart, alcohol-laden liquid, she pushed the jug away.

"You—" she sputtered as Wade set the bottle down, but before she could say more, he pushed her back to lie on the blanket and claimed her lips as he covered her body with his own.

Ashby felt her head spin—from the alcohol or Wade's kiss? She didn't know and didn't care. She filled her senses with the taste of apples blending on their tongues, the weight of him pressing against her swelling breasts and the feel of the hard muscles in his back beneath her fingers.

Wade's blood pounded in his veins as the passion hidden beneath their banter burst the bonds of control. A remnant of rational thought made him roll to his side and pull her with him to keep from crushing her. He cradled her neck with one arm, while sliding his free hand down over the curve of her waist and hip, then up her back to press the softness of her breasts harder against his chest.

No ridge of a bra strap interrupted the smooth path of his fingers. Instead, he felt the slick glide of satin beneath the cotton of her T-shirt, inflaming his senses further as his imagination painted a vivid picture of her clad in nothing but her lingerie.

Massaging the ridges of her spine with his thumb, he moved his hand down her back toward her waistband. He ached with the desire to touch her bare skin. What little worry he felt about anyone stumbling upon them behind their screen of bushes added to his mounting excitement. Dizzy with the thrill of the chase, the fear of discovery, the lure of the unknown, he felt himself surrender to the woman in his arms as she surrendered to him.

Ashby was beyond thought. Drunk with desire, with the taste of Wade and apples, she pulled her mouth from his to explore the strong pillar of his neck with her lips as her shoulders writhed and her back arched in response to the sensual pressure of his hand on her back.

Wade reached her waistband to find her shirt already pulled free by the stretching of her arms about his neck. Slipping his hand beneath the cotton to caress the underlying satin, he gently tugged it upward only to discover that it had no end. It was, he realized dimly, a full slip.

His fever to touch her flesh growing, he slid his hand up and under her shirt to caress the smooth skin between her shoulder blades. Yet still he burned, half maddened by her soft nibbles on his neck and by her breasts, which rubbed against his chest as he stroked her back. Abandoning all decorum, he slipped his hand across the sleek fabric of the front of her slip to cup her breast.

"Wade." A vague memory of where they were brought protest to Ashby's lips, but his mouth covered hers as his thumb found the taut nipple thrusting at its satin confinement.

Powerless to resist the touch she craved, Ashby protested no more as he pushed her slip aside and covered her bare breast with his callused palm.

"Howdy, folks!"

Wade and Ashby stiffened and sprang apart before either realized that what they heard was a man's voice amplified by a microphone. No one stood over them.

"Welcome to Clairmont's Independence Day Fair! Are you having a g-o-o-o-d time?"

"I was," Wade muttered, watching Ashby sit up and tuck her shirt back into her waistband. His disgruntled tone of voice rang in sharp contrast to the happy cheers and clapping that answered the announcer's voice from the rest of the field. The magic of the moment broken, he didn't dare reach for her again.

Ashby heard Wade's response, but kept her head down, mortified by her behavior. Here she was, nearly thirty-five years old, a mature, sophisticated woman, and she'd lain on a blanket and necked in public with Wade like a hormone-crazed teenager!

"Well, we've got some more good times coming up for you," the announcer continued.

"I certainly hope so," Wade said more cheerfully. Ashby's head snapped up. He grinned at her glare.

"First on our agenda," the amplified voice boomed, "is our very own dueling-banjo team, Abe Hanlon and Jake Evans!"

"Time to dance." Wade grabbed Ashby's hand and hauled her to her feet. Eager to escape the scene of her debauchery, Ashby allowed him to lead her toward the bandstand.

Wade nodded to other couples gathering on the same grassy area. He grinned down at Ashby and slipped an arm around her slim waist, but she held herself rigid, her gaze glued to the two men onstage. Their banjos twanged as the men made a ceremony of tuning the instruments and taunting one another.

She looked, Wade decided, quite thoroughly kissed and not very happy about it. He supposed he should apologize—he hadn't intended to go as far as he had—but he couldn't bring himself to regret anything other

than that they hadn't been in a more private place.
She'd been his for the taking and she knew it as well as
he did. That was the reason for her chagrin. He grinned
again.

Their banjos tuned, the two musicians began playing. Wade swayed to the beat, but Ashby stood mo-
tionless. "Just stomp your feet," he said, bending down
to speak in her ear. "The rest comes naturally. Even to
a city slicker."

"I don't want to dance." She wanted to leave, wanted
to go home to Georgetown, where she knew who and
what she was—where she was in control and safe.

"Dance or I'll haul you back to that blanket and finish what we started."

"I'll scream."

"Not for long." He grinned and she longed to slap the
smug self-satisfaction off his face. Instead, she lifted one
foot, then the other. Wade did likewise and she noticed
how lightly he moved despite his size. The beat quick-
ened gradually, as the performers strove to outdo one
another, one banjo answering the other. Swept up by
the music and the energy of the dancers around them,
Ashby kicked off her shoes and twirled her skirt.

She hadn't danced or listened to bluegrass music in
years, but she remembered it well. And the demand of
matching the beat kept her from thinking—a welcome
relief from the confusion swirling in her brain. Her head
held high, she met Wade's gaze, her expression chal-
lenging as she increased her tempo. His steps quick-
ened, too, and soon their private duel matched the pace
set by the competing banjos.

Wade laughed with surprise as Ashby danced circles
around him. Her small feet flying, her skirt flaring
about her slim legs, she moved to the music as if she'd

been born to it. And, he supposed, she had. But he hadn't expected her to like it. Not only had she kicked off her shoes, but her blue eyes sparkled with delight and her curls had escaped their sleek styling. He couldn't believe this was the same sophisticated creature who'd driven a Porsche into Hickory.

As the banjos crescendoed, he caught her in his arms and spun her in circles, not setting her down until the last note faded away. When her feet touched the ground, he stole a light kiss.

"You just keep your mind on dancing, like your Aunt Dessie told you," Ashby said, standing on tiptoe to speak in his ear so he could hear her over the applause for the musicians.

Wade grinned but made no promises as the next piece started and he moved with the music. Ashby followed suit, determined to dance until she dropped rather than return to the privacy of their blanket. She was too susceptible to his touch and couldn't trust herself alone with him—not unless she believed there was hope for the future.

She pictured him at one of her art-show openings, his masculinity enhanced rather than tamed by a tuxedo. All the other men would look like the effeminate snobs they were.

What? She caught herself. She'd never before thought of the men at her art gallery as unmanly or patronizing. Wade's effect on her was scrambling her brain.

"Okay, cuz, where's the applejack?"

Ashby turned to find four of Wade's cousins behind her. Wade shrugged and kept dancing.

"It's on a blanket behind those bushes," she answered, pointing the way and hoping they'd drink it all.

Her fantasy of Wade in a tuxedo at an art show shifted to show him at the bar drinking out of bottles rather than glasses. He was, she reminded herself, long on looks but short on social graces.

"Oh, no, you don't," Wade warned his cousins as they turned in the direction she'd indicated. They ignored him and kept walking. "For a little woman, you have a big mouth," he added, taking her hand and dragging her after the four men. Ashby resisted long enough to pick up her shoes, but he gave her no time to put them on.

"What happened to your bottle?" he demanded, when they reached the blanket and found his cousins happily passing the jug. Ashby slipped on her shoes, then sat down, pleased at the opportunity to rest in the safety of company. Their names all started with a *J*, she remembered. Jeff, Jim, John and Jack. They were big like Wade, but their dark hair didn't seem to have the same ebony sheen nor their eyes the same deep emerald hue.

"Mom caught us letting the young 'uns have some and she took it," Jack answered.

"Aunt Dessie?" Wade grinned as he joined them on the blanket. "And you couldn't get it back?"

"Old habits are hard to break." All four of them broke into a chorus of Yes, ma'ams and No, ma'ams.

"Did she give you whippings when you were small?" Ashby asked with a meaningful glance at Wade.

"With a hickory switch," Jeff replied, grimacing and rubbing his backside. "And she'd still do it if she could catch us!"

"Gave my wife one with a big red bow tied on it when I got married," the oldest one, Jim, said amid hoots of laughter from the others. "I'm careful to give her no cause to use it." He offered Ashby the jug.

Her dancing had made her thirsty and she didn't want to seem unfriendly, so Ashby took it, keeping a wary eye on Wade. "Don't let him tilt the bottle," she directed before taking a small sip.

"Trying to get her drunk?" Jeff asked Wade. "You must be losing your touch."

"I'd settle for getting her alone," Wade growled and reached for the bottle, the contents of which had dropped considerably. Jeff whisked it from Ashby's hands.

"Think that was a hint to leave?" he asked his brothers.

"Naw. We're his favorite relatives," John answered.

"Could be," Jack suggested.

"We'll make a fair trade," Jeff decided, standing. "He gets to keep his woman and we keep the applejack."

"Deal," Wade agreed and rose to his feet with the others. "But I get one drink first."

The brothers pretended to consult one another with much scratching of their heads and rubbing of their chins. Wade rolled his eyes. "Okay," Jeff announced and passed the jug to John, then leaned down to pick up Ashby. "But we hold the little lady hostage."

Ashby laughed and wrapped her arms around Jeff's neck. Their horseplay reminded her of her own brothers. Wade scowled, but took the jug. Her eyes widened as she watched the amount he drank. The brothers had already consumed nearly half the bottle and by the time Wade handed it back to them, the level had dropped another inch.

"Okay, give her back." Wade held out his arms.

"Just put me down," she said hurriedly, but Jeff stepped forward and handed her over to Wade.

"I'm not a sack of potatoes," Ashby objected, but Wade held her easily as he bade a pointed farewell to his cousins.

"You're going to need someone to drive you home, the amount you drank."

She'd meant to speak sharply, but somehow the words came out tinged with a gentle concern as she found a soft spot on his shoulder to rest her head. Acutely aware of the strength of the arms supporting her, she inhaled the heady, male scent of him—the aromas of a woodsy cologne and soap blended with the light sheen of moisture on his skin; the same scent, she was sure, that would cling to him in the aftermath of loving.... She closed her eyes in anticipation of another of his apple-flavored kisses.

"If that's an offer," he said as he set her down, his impersonal touch wrenching her out of her sensual fog, "I'll take you up on it later. But I'm hungry again. Let's go check out the desserts." He bent and set aside the untouched bag of peanuts, then picked up the blanket and shook it. "Get the nuts, will ya?" he added, slinging the blanket over his shoulder as he strode away.

Ashby stared at his broad back. "You," she muttered, "can drive over a cliff, for all I care!"

6

WINCING AS HE WALKED away, Wade tugged the blanket over his shoulder so it hung past his thighs to hide the evidence of the ache in his groin. He wouldn't, he swore, touch that little package of blond dynamite again until they were alone. His reaction to her wasn't safe, wasn't decent—and definitely wasn't for public viewing.

The way she'd nestled against his chest, her body soft and pliant in his arms, the little sigh that had escaped her lips—all had told him she'd wanted him to kiss her again. But he hadn't dared kiss her, hadn't trusted himself to be able to stop.

The dry rustle of peanuts against a paper bag told him that Ashby had caught up with him and he risked a sideways glance at her. She walked with her small chin held high, her eyes fixed straight ahead and every line of her petite body held rigid. Her arms and legs moved in wooden synchronization, the swing of her hand shaking the peanuts.

First, she'd been furious at herself for responding to his kiss. Now she was mad because he hadn't kissed her! She was, he decided, more confused than he was. At least he could admit he wanted her, but she couldn't bring herself to acknowledge a similar need.

She would eventually, he promised himself. He wouldn't touch her again until she did. He could seduce her body, but he wanted her mind to be as willing. And for that, she would have to make a conscious decision. He would wait and stalk her with the patience of a wild animal hunting its prey. The pursuit, begun as much to please his family as himself, was now strictly personal.

By the time they reached the picnic grounds, Wade was whistling, which made Ashby want to scream with frustration. She spotted Anna at a picnic table and headed in her direction without a word to Wade. She couldn't bear to be with him one more minute. He ran hot and cold, as she'd feared, and she simply couldn't take it.

Wade's cousin greeted her with a smile as Ashby tossed the peanuts on the table and took the empty seat on the bench beside her. A tall, gaunt man with thinning hair and friendly brown eyes reached around her to shake Ashby's hand and introduce himself as her husband, John.

"Anna here tells me you want to put her quilts in a fancy gallery," he said and Ashby nodded, pleased that Anna had talked to her husband immediately.

"But you want to give her some kind of contract 'stead of cash?" John added bluntly.

"I run my gallery on a consignment and commission basis," Ashby explained. "I can't tie up my working capital by buying exhibits outright. I invest my money in advertising, catering for special showings where I invite my best—and wealthiest—customers and, of course, for the gallery itself." She smiled. "Real estate in Georgetown is not cheap."

"Neither are Porsches," Wade murmured, his lips brushing her ear as he sat down next to her. She stiffened, wondering what he had against her car. She darted an irritable glance at him as his hard thigh pressed against the softness of her own.

All four of them sat with their backs to the picnic table, looking at the carnival, but Wade made himself the most comfortable. He stretched his legs out in front of him and propped his elbows back on the table, brushing her arm and grinning engagingly as he did so.

"Since I want you to hold your finished quilts through the summer—" Ashby turned her back on Wade and spoke to Anna "—I'm willing to take a forty-percent commission instead of my usual fifty." What had made her say that? she wondered, surprised at herself. Did she want to impress Wade with her generosity? No. Yes. Maybe a little. But mostly, she thought, it was the hope and pride in Anna's blue eyes. And the skepticism in John's brown ones.

Her offer would cut her profit margin considerably, but she found she didn't care. She wanted Anna's quilts. This exhibit was becoming increasingly important to her. Was it guilt at having turned her back on her roots? She shrugged inwardly. The reason didn't matter. She knew instinctively that the folk art, so different from the usual fare in Georgetown galleries, could be a success; she'd come to trust her instincts as much as her business acumen.

John looked at his wife, then turned back to Ashby. "She done all the work. I reckon the decision's up to her."

Anna's smile gave Ashby her answer. "You won't be sorry," she promised the older woman as she found her purse and pulled out a pen. Anna dug the contract out of her pocket.

"Handshake's good enough in these parts," John said, as Anna wrote her name and Ashby adjusted her commission and countersigned.

"I know," Ashby spoke softly, touched by their faith in her. "But my accountant will kill me if I don't follow his rules!" John chuckled and invited Wade to join him in a game of horseshoes as she handed Anna her copy of the contract.

Wade rose with John, but a swarm of children surrounded them. "Uncle Wade," they begged, waving sticks of all shapes and sizes at him, "please make us some toys!"

"May as well say yes," John advised as he extricated himself. "You know they won't leave you alone until you do."

"Uncle?" Ashby asked as Wade sat down again. "Do you have brothers and sisters I haven't met?"

"No, I was an only child." Wade patted the heads of the boys and girls nearest him. "These guys are actually a collection of second and third cousins, but they call me uncle because I'm bigger than they are."

"These are my Barbara's," Anna said proudly, pulling two towheaded toddlers into her lap. "Matthew and Kristin. I was a grandmother at thirty-eight. Guess that's what I get for starting a family right out of high school 'stead of going to art school like I'd planned."

Ashby looked for, but couldn't see, a trace of regret on the other woman's face. She admired the peace she sensed behind her words. Anna hadn't followed her youthful dreams, but she'd found happiness in the turn her life had taken.

Her own arms ached with emptiness as she stared at the small children in Anna's lap. Would she give up her gallery for them? No. And neither would Anna give up her family for a career as an artist. But her exhibit would give Anna the professional recognition for her talent her life had thus far lacked. Secretly crossing her fingers, Ashby prayed that she, too, could combine the best of both worlds someday.

"You didn't get the giggles when John kissed you," Wade teased Anna as he pulled out a pocketknife and whittled at the stick her grandson gave him. The other children milled about and mumbled among themselves as they waited their turn.

Anna laughed. "I sure didn't! Guess if I had, I might've been an artist. But then I might be like you, with nothing but cousins 'stead of my own kids." She glanced at Wade slyly. "Not that it's too late for some, mind you."

Wade didn't respond to Anna's remark as he handed her grandson a stick transformed into a marching soldier. A fork in the branch had been turned into two legs and small side branches trimmed into arms.

None of the edges left were sharp, but Wade was firm as he warned the child that he'd take the toy back if he caught him poking or hitting another child with it. Matthew nodded obediently as he climbed down from his grandmother's lap, the soldier clutched in one hand.

Wade would make a good father, Ashby mused. With his air of command, he wouldn't need a hickory stick to maintain discipline. Nor would he leave the child rearing to his wife.

"Now, if you'd let Kay have a baby like she wanted when you moved here," Anna said, "maybe you'd have your own family."

"Kay wasn't happy here," Wade replied without looking up from his carving. "Better that she was free to leave. A baby wouldn't have made a difference."

"You don't know women," Anna countered.

Concentrating on his whittling, Wade didn't answer immediately. Another toy soldier had taken shape in his hands. Like magic, Ashby thought, as enthralled as the children. A twig on the side of this branch had been shaped to look like an arm raised in salute.

He handed it to Anna's granddaughter with the same admonishment to be careful. Kristin gurgled happily and chased after her brother.

"I knew Kay," he said curtly.

"Where did she go?" Ashby asked, seizing the opening Anna had provided. Guessing that her question trespassed on the part of the past he'd silently declared off-limits when they sat under the tree by the river, she held her breath in hopes that he'd answer.

"Back to Chicago." He glanced up at her, as if sensing the weight of her stare as she willed him to tell her more.

"She was a stock trader, a career woman. Like you." He lowered his gaze as he resumed his whittling. "A house in the country had been a nice dream, but the reality of it bored her. She missed the excitement of the Board of Trade, the competition, the drive." He shrugged. "You can get as addicted to your own adrenaline rush as any drug."

"And what did you do in Chicago?" Ashby asked, suspecting that he spoke from experience. Although her attention was on Wade, she felt Anna rise and leave them alone.

"The same."

"But you don't miss it?"

"I don't have a choice." He didn't look up as he transformed more sticks into figures with deft, efficient cuts of his knife and gave them to the dwindling group of children.

"Why?"

He stopped whittling and returned her steady gaze, his expression guarded. "It's a long story." He bent his head close to her ear and spoke in a low voice, so only she could hear. "Come home with me tonight and I'll tell you."

Ashby averted her face and bit the tip of her tongue. He'd opened a door to his past that would explain why he refused to sell his furniture, but it wasn't the art-gallery owner that wanted to say yes; it was the woman.

"Do you have etchings to show me, too?" she asked lightly, if somewhat breathlessly.

He didn't move, didn't pull back. Barely an inch separated them as he allowed his gaze to linger on her lips. When he spoke, his apple-scented breath fanned her cheek.

"No, but I do have other furniture I've made."

Her head snapped back. "You don't play fair!"

He grinned. "All's fair in love and war."

"And is this love?" She held his gaze as she waited for his answer, determined not to be the one to look away first.

His grin faded as he studied her. "Is there a difference?" He turned away, giving yet another toy soldier away and reaching for the last stick held by a small girl he called Becky.

"I don't see a soldier in this one," he said, fingering Becky's piece of wood thoughtfully. "I think I see a ballerina, just like you plan to be. Would you like that?"

Her head spinning from Wade's cynical words about love, Ashby felt as if she watched from a distance as

Becky squealed with delight and clapped her hands excitedly. His wife had hurt him deeply.

When the rough-hewn ballerina was safe in Becky's hands and she'd left them alone at the table, Wade slipped an arm around Ashby's shoulders. "Do you believe in love?" he asked.

"Yes." She paused, wondering if there was such a thing as love at first sight. Was that why his slightest touch rocked her like a tree buffeted by winds of hurricane force?

From the first moment she'd laid eyes on him, he'd impressed her with his strength, his quiet competence. A good provider. Intelligent. A strong sense of family. All the qualities she'd want in a husband. But they'd argued from the first moment they'd met. Was that what he meant by love and war?

"And I think there's a difference between love and war," she added more uncertainly.

"Prove it to me," he challenged. "Come away with me for a few days. I'll take you to parts of West Virginia you've never seen. The state is called the Switzerland of America for a reason, you know." He spoke in a low, deliberately seductive voice, but he felt a trace of uneasiness at the thought that his lighthearted game could turn serious.

"Yeah, it's all mountains," Ashby muttered, playing for time. Was he admitting there was the potential for love between them?

"And the most beautiful places are accessible only with four-wheel drive. I know where there's a crystal-clear mountain pond complete with a sandy beach and a waterfall we could have all to ourselves. We could camp and swim and not wear a stitch of clothes for days." Adding the persuasion of his touch, he trailed a fingertip up her neck and into her hair.

Ashby repressed a shudder at the tingling his light caress sparked through her body. "I don't know," she murmured honestly, resting her head in his big hand as she turned to face him. "I'm not sure you're good for me."

He grinned and again brought his face close to hers, his green eyes warm with promises of sensual delight. "Oh, I'd be good for you, all right."

For how long? she asked silently as she stared back at him. *And what happens if I want more than a summer romance? What if I fall in love with you?*

The clatter of dishes on the table behind them shattered their silent communion. Ashby raised her head and Wade dropped his hand to her shoulder as he swung around to face the table.

"Dessert," Anna announced cheerfully. "Or did you two lovebirds have something sweeter in mind?"

"Yes," Wade growled, sure that Ashby had been about to agree.

"No," Ashby said and jumped up, eager to escape the intimacy of the moment with Wade. He was moving too fast for her. "Let me help. Those banana cream pies look wonderful!"

Anna looked at her cousin, then smiled at Ashby. "You jes' set right back down," she said. "Everything is under control."

Ashby sank back into her seat unwillingly. Anna's allegiance was clear; there'd be no escape from Wade in that direction. Or in any direction, she realized as the afternoon wore on. Wade remained at her side as fixedly as a Seeing Eye dog, and his relatives encouraged him. If she moved from one table to another, two places were made for them to sit, even if someone else had to stand.

Judging from the knowing glances shot in their direction and the frequency of people nudging one another's sides with their elbows, she guessed that Wade hadn't dated much since his wife had left him. The thought was comforting. Despite the bold way he'd propositioned her, he apparently wasn't a womanizer.

As the glow of the late-afternoon sun faded into dusk, everyone began packing up to move across the river and find a good seat for the Fourth of July fireworks display. "I'll take Ashby home," Wade told Coot. "We haven't ridden any of the rides yet. They're more fun at night." He winked at his grandfather, but turned a straight face to Ashby. "Because of all the pretty lights."

Which home? Ashby wondered, sure he had more up his sleeve than the carnival rides. *His or Coot's?* The decision was hers and she could avoid it by leaving with Coot and Millie, but she wanted to stay. She'd promised herself all the rides and candy she'd had to deny herself as a child.

And, she added silently, despite her disconcerting awareness of Wade's slightest touch, she'd enjoyed his company throughout the afternoon. He was a good conversationalist, always including a quick explanation if he or his relatives touched on subjects unfamiliar to her.

"Need a couple of bucks to slip the Ferris-wheel driver to stop you up top?" Coot asked Wade, winking broadly and jabbing him in the ribs with his elbow. "So you can see the fireworks," he explained, turning an innocent face to Ashby.

Wade laughed. "No, I think I have enough." He took Ashby's arm and steered her toward the carnival. "We'll see you later."

"Let's start with the swings," Ashby said, pulling him in that direction and choosing to ignore Coot's teasing.

"Saving the Ferris wheel for last?" Wade taunted.

"Absolutely," she agreed merrily. "I'm going to spend all your money before we get to it!"

She almost succeeded. First, Wade thought he'd never get her off the swings. They were, he discovered, a childhood favorite. And, childlike, she insisted on the outermost swing, "because it flew the highest and fastest."

Not content with the mechanized speed of the ride, she kicked her legs to make her seat swing higher and twirled it in circles until the chains unwound of their own accord. To her delighted surprise, Wade readily complied with her instructions to do the same.

Once off the swings, she begged for gaudy items at every pitchman's tent. Wade found himself tossing quarters, throwing darts and shooting imitation rifles at every imaginable target from floating ducks to water-filled balloons. He'd always considered the games fixed and a waste of money, but the pleasure on Ashby's face was worth every penny.

When he won a blue teddy bear with a lopsided grin and crossed eyes, she hugged him. "I dreamed about doing this as a kid," she confessed. "You can't know what it was like to come to places like this and have to choose one or two rides and eat a peanut butter and jelly sandwich instead of candy."

Wade stared down at her upturned face, seeing the earnestness in her big blue eyes. "So we're making up for lost time?" he asked and raised one hand to stroke her soft cheek.

She nodded. "Do you mind terribly? I really shouldn't be spending all your money. Let me pay you back." Attacked by guilt, she stuffed the teddy bear under her arm and delved into the shoulder purse again strung between her breasts.

"No way." His hands caught hers. "I can afford it and I've never had such a good time at a carnival."

Kay, he remembered, had thought country fairs dirty and country music low-class. He'd expected Ashby to feel the same way. But this was a moment out of time and place for her, he reminded himself, an escapade with no bearing on the reality of their differences. It changed nothing. They'd enjoy their time together, part amicably, and he'd be free to feign a broken heart and win a reprieve from his family's incessant matchmaking.

Ashby studied his face, suddenly feeling shy and a little ridiculous. Was he secretly laughing at her?

He leaned down and brushed her lips with his as if sensing her need for reassurance. "I've always had this thing for merry-go-rounds," he confessed in a stage whisper, resuming their playfulness. He raised his head and glanced around as though afraid of being overheard.

"Really?" Ashby grinned, relieved to hear that he was enjoying himself and not making fun of her. "Let's go!"

The stirrups were too high for Wade's long legs and he had to bend his knees every time the horse dipped, but he whooped with gusto whenever his mount lifted his feet off the floor. Ashby teased him unmercifully and laughed until her sides ached. No other man she'd known would have risked his dignity by riding a merry-go-round with her. Nor would she normally risk her own.

"You look ridiculous carrying that blue teddy bear," Wade informed her in retaliation for her teasing as the ride ended and they dismounted.

"I think I'll name him after you." Ashby held the bear at arm's length and studied it. "Whenever I look at it, I'll think of you on that little horse. Wade, Jr. What do you think?"

Wade swung his arm around her shoulders and pulled her close to his side. "I think I'd prefer to have the pleasure of siring my own juniors."

"Does that mean you're ready for the Ferris wheel?" Ashby asked lightly.

Wade grinned. "Normally, I'd prefer to do my siring in a more private place, but—" he stroked his chin thoughtfully "—it's about time for the fireworks to start and making love in a moving Ferris wheel could be a challenge."

Ashby poked him in the ribs. "Ferris wheels are for necking only."

"And did you do a lot of that?"

"Only when my parents and brothers stayed home— which wasn't often!"

As they approached their seat on the Ferris wheel, she saw Wade slip money into the operator's hand and point upward. Choking back a laugh, she cleared her throat and tried to look demure as the operator glanced at her, then grinned at Wade and gave him a thumbs-up sign.

She'd set her purse on one side of her and the teddy bear on the seat between them, but Wade set it on her lap as soon as he sat down. He put his arm around her and pulled her close as the Ferris wheel moved upward.

"We're too old for this," she said, but snuggled up to him, anyway.

"Never too old for merry-go-rounds and Ferris wheels," he murmured, cupping her face in one large hand and lowering his mouth to hers.

This kiss was gentle, sweet with affection and shared good humor. Ashby gave herself up to it without reserve. Wade clung to the feelings of tenderness she'd elicited from him, but when her lips parted beneath his, he plunged his tongue into the moist velvet of her mouth.

Oblivious to the shrieks of other passengers or to the revolving of the Ferris wheel, they allowed the kiss to deepen until the wheel lurched to a stop at the top of its rotation, bringing them back to reality.

The lights of the carnival twinkled below them, but Ashby laid her head on Wade's shoulder and stared up at the sky. "The stars are so much brighter in the country than in the city," she murmured. "I feel like I could reach out and touch them." A feeling, she suspected, that had more to do with Wade's kiss than with their position so high in the sky.

"Especially now," Wade said, pointing across the river as the first of the fireworks flared over the town and a kaleidoscope of colors exploded against the black night.

Ashby clapped her hands excitedly. "What perfect timing! How long will the operator let us sit here?"

"If it's not long enough, I'll pay for another ride."

"This really is special," Ashby said, looking up at him with shining eyes. "I can't thank you enough."

"You're welcome." Wade smiled down at her for a moment, then pressed his lips against the top of her head. "Do you have any idea what you do to me?" he asked her.

"I have a fair idea." She smiled and rubbed her cheek on his shoulder, then lifted her face to his again. "Because you do the same thing to me."

Wade caught his breath at her admission, but didn't speak. He was afraid to—afraid he'd break the spell and scare her off again.

She raised her hand and ran a fingertip across his lips. "So when do we go camping?"

Take 4 Medical Romances

Mills & Boon Medical Romances capture all the excitement and emotion of a busy medical world... A world, however, where love and romance are never far away.

We will send you 4 MEDICAL ROMANCES absolutely FREE plus a cuddly teddy bear and a mystery gift, as your introduction to this superb series.

At the same time we'll reserve a subscription for you to our Reader Service.

Every month you could receive the 4 latest Medical Romances delivered direct to your door postage and packing FREE, plus a free Newsletter filled with competitions, author news and much more.

And remember there's no obligation, you may cancel or suspend your subscription at any time. So you've nothing to lose and a world of romance to gain!

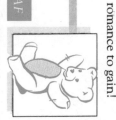

FREE

FILL IN THE FREE BOOKS COUPON OVERLEAF

Your Free Gifts!

Return this card, and we'll send you a lovely little soft brown bear together with a mystery gift... So don't delay!

NO STAMP NEEDED

FREE BOOKS COUPON

YES Please send me 4 FREE Medical Romances together with my teddy bear and mystery gift. Please also reserve a special Reader Service subscription for me. If I decide to subscribe, I will receive 4 brand new books for just £6.40 each month, postage and packing free. If, however, I decide not to subscribe, I shall write to you within 10 days. The free books and gifts will be mine to keep in anycase. I understand that I am under no obligation - I may cancel or suspend my subscription at any time simply by writing to you. I am over 18 years of age.

EXTRA BONUS

We all love mysteries, so as well as the FREE books and Teddy, here's an intriguing gift especially for you. No clues - send off today!

12A2D

Ms/Mrs/Miss/Mr _____

Address _____

_____

Postcode _____ Signature _____

One per household. Offer expires 31st January 1993. The right is reserved to refuse an application and change the terms of this offer. Readers in Southern Africa write to Book Services International Ltd., P.O. Box 41654, Craighall, Transvaal 2024. Other Overseas and Eire, send for details. You may be mailed with other offers from other reputable companies as a result of this application. If you would prefer not to share in this opportunity, please tick box. ☐

mps MAILING PREFERENCE SERVICE

Reader Service
FREEPOST
P.O. Box 236
Croydon
CR9 9EL

SEND NO MONEY NOW

7

"Camping? You!"

At her sister's shriek of laughter, Ashby held the telephone receiver away from her ear. She'd woken that morning struck by the enormity of what she had done. In Wade's company, all she'd thought about was the prospect of spending time alone with him. But camping? In the wild? Without so much as an outlet for her electric toothbrush? Or her blow dryer?

"We'll wait to be together," Wade had said, when he brought her home to Coot and Millie's house after the carnival, "until we have days instead of hours. I don't want to have to check in with my mother in the morning so she won't worry about you." And then he'd chuckled. "And you might want to change your mind."

She'd assured him she wouldn't, then slept soundly, warmed inside and out by the memory of his kisses. But she'd woken not only to daylight but to reality. Somehow, she'd managed to get through a huge breakfast of pancakes and sausage with Millie and Coot, then asked to use their telephone in the privacy of the living room.

In times of crisis, she always turned to Sue. She could see her now, seated at her breakfast bar, her feet propped up on the adjacent bar stool, the brown curls she encouraged rather than tamed tumbling down her shoulders. As she waited for her sister to overcome her hysterics, she congratulated herself on thinking to use her telephone credit card. It would likely be a long conversation.

"Sorry." Sue stifled one last giggle and Ashby cautiously returned the receiver to her ear. "Tell me this again. Miss Priss is going *camping?*"

"It seemed like a good idea at the time." Ashby gritted her teeth at the reminder of the nickname she'd earned as a teenager. With the arrival of adolescence, she'd put her tomboy days behind her and begged to exchange her blue jeans for dresses. Climbing trees and playing football with brothers, she'd been certain, were not pastimes of the models and actresses she'd longed to emulate.

"I *have* to meet this man!"

"One matchmaking family is enough, thank you," Ashby said hastily. "That's not why I'm calling. I need help. How do I get out of this?"

"Why would you want to get out of it? The man sounds like an absolute dreamboat!"

He is, Ashby silently agreed. "Because a luxury resort in the Bahamas is more my style!" she wailed. "Because I can't even brush my teeth without electricity! Because I don't have anything to wear!"

"Buy a regular toothbrush, and it doesn't sound like you'll need much in the way of clothes."

"Sue . . ." Ashby's voice was laden with the urge to strangle her cheerful sister.

"What do you want me to say?" Sue answered reasonably. "You want to go or else you wouldn't have said you would. So go and have a good time."

"But I barely know the man!"

"I think you know him better than you think you do."

"Are we back to biological clocks and hormones?"

"Something indefinable. Remember when Tom and I met? We were both seriously involved with other people, yet we couldn't stay away from one another. No matter how civilized and intellectualized the human race gets, there is something instinctive that happens when you meet your mate."

"Wade can't be my mate. He's totally wrong for me."

"That's your head talking. Just because he lives on a mountain in West Virginia doesn't mean you can't be in love with him."

"But he's also cynical, arrogant and only interested in an affair!"

"Since when did you ever choose an easy goal? You could have settled for working in a gallery instead of owning your own," Sue reminded her. "And you also mentioned that he's gorgeous, has a great sense of humor, is close to his family and good with kids. What else could you want?"

"To know he's thinking about love as well as lust."

Ashby felt a moment of grim satisfaction at giving her sister pause. Silence reigned for a moment, then Sue spoke more slowly.

"I think you worry about the future too much. You've planned your life from *A* to *Z* since you were eighteen. It's time to let go and listen to your instincts. Remember Tom's brother, Alan? One gorgeous hunk of man that was also witty, intelligent and a talented, professional photographer—who wanted to marry you badly. He traveled, accepted your career and wanted a family, but did you melt when he touched you?

"No, sirree." Sue didn't wait for Ashby's answer. "But you do when Wade does. Go on this camping trip and find out what it means. You owe it to yourself."

"One last, wild fling before I settle into spinster-hood?" Ashby asked wryly.

"Your *only* wild fling. If that's how you want to think of it, fine. Just do it!"

She should have known Sue would tell her to go for it, Ashby mused as she hung up the phone a short time later. Was that why she'd called her? Because she wanted to be persuaded that she was making the right decision?

She shrugged. Her older sister was right again. She had planned her life for the past seventeen years and she faced the prospect of spending the rest of it alone. All the more reason to allow herself this grand passion. No man had ever affected her like Wade. *Overwhelmed* might be a better word, she amended wryly.

She'd been able to fit other men into the social cate-gory of her life and keep them there, where they didn't interfere with her work or her sleep. Whereas Wade made her feel like a starry-eyed adolescent content to spend her days and nights daydreaming about him.

"Millie?" she called as she made her way to the kitchen. "Where can I buy a pair of blue jeans?"

"Fashionable or practical?"

"Both." Ashby grinned. She didn't see why she couldn't go camping and still look good, but her grin faded as she realized that Millie had cleaned the kitchen. "I told you I'd take care of the dishes."

"There weren't many and you insisted on paying room and board," Millie reminded her. Before they'd left for the fair the previous morning, Ashby had prac-tically forced money on her. "Now you're not only a guest, but a paying guest."

Ashby sank down onto a chair at the kitchen table and ran a hand through her hair, which she'd yet to straighten. "You wouldn't let me pay half the going rate of a motel and you're feeding me, too." They'd already gone through this argument. Millie's smiling intransigence was a feminine version of Wade's muleheaded stubbornness.

"You can do the dinner dishes," Millie said, apparently recognizing the frustration on Ashby's face. She poured two cups of coffee, brought them to the table and sat down. "Now that nosy old Coot's over at the store, let's have a woman-to-woman talk. Did you have a nice time with Wade last night?"

"Yes," Ashby admitted and smiled as Millie beamed. "As soon as he can arrange for someone to look after the farm, we're going camping." She prayed that she wasn't blushing and hurried on. "Which is why I need a pair of blue jeans. Can you think of anything else I'll need?"

"Shorts and a swimsuit. Maybe a sweatshirt. The nights in these mountains can still be cool." Millie smiled slyly. "Although I expect Wade will keep you warm enough."

Ashby choked on her coffee and felt her cheeks flame. Millie laughed.

"No call to be embarrassed, girl! I couldn't be happier. You two are old enough to know what you're doing."

Ashby stared into her coffee cup, wishing she could be as certain about that, but kept silent. She raised her head, then gently clinked her cup against Millie's in a silent toast. "So where's the best place to go shopping?"

IN THE KITCHEN of his farm, Wade was talking to Samson. The big black dog sat at his feet, his brown eyes fixed in rapt attention upon his master . . . and on the untouched bowl of oatmeal on the table in front of him.

"I thought I had it all figured out," Wade was saying, "and then she had to go and turn the tables on me. She was dancing barefoot, for crissakes!" Samson whined sympathetically.

"Ms. Hoity-Toity Art-Gallery Owner, sexy, sophisticated lady, riding those swings and the merry-go-round like a kid in seventh heaven. Then she looks up at me with those big blue eyes and says, 'So when are we going camping?' Just who is in charge here?" He glared down at the dog. Samson slunk down to his belly and laid his head on his paws, no longer eyeing the hot cereal.

Wade pushed away from the table. He had no appetite and it was all *her* fault. He'd fallen under her spell and if he wasn't careful, the little blonde would have him eating out of her hand and he wouldn't have to fake a broken heart when she left him.

He strode into the bathroom, faced the mirror and opened his flannel shirt and stared at the faint white line down the middle of his chest, barely visible beneath the mat of dark hair: the line that had divided his life into black and white, with no shades of gray.

She didn't know about that, but he did. And he couldn't, wouldn't forget it. He'd enjoy her company, enjoy getting to know her and—he grinned as he buttoned up his shirt—he'd enjoy making love with her. No more, no less.

His peace of mind restored, he returned to the kitchen. Samson was again in a sitting position by his chair, his nose level with the table as he gazed longingly at the cereal bowl.

"You can have it," Wade told him and set the bowl on the floor. For some reason, he still didn't feel hungry.

WHEN WADE PULLED UP in front of his family's house a week later, Ashby was outfitted not only with blue jeans, sweatshirts, tennis shoes, shorts and bathing suits, but also a bad case of nerves.

She hadn't seen him since the carnival. He'd called to tell her when to be ready and to warn her to wear casual clothes. But his voice had been matter-of-fact, even brisk, without any of the sensual overtones he'd used when they'd initially discussed the trip. She hadn't heard from him since.

The farm kept him busy, Millie assured her, when she caught her gazing longingly at the telephone. During the day, Ashby occupied herself shopping and looking for crafts for her exhibit. She found a woman who made teddy bears, which she wasn't sure should be considered folk art, but she couldn't resist them. As beautiful as they were, however, none could ever be as precious to her as the cross-eyed blue one Wade had won for her.

She clung to that bear every night, needing its reminder of how close she'd felt to Wade at the carnival. When she was alone in the dark, the idea of going off into the boondocks with a man who couldn't even be bothered to call her didn't seem like the brightest idea she'd ever had.

Nor did she feel reassured when she picked up her small but stuffed suitcase and followed a smug Coot and a smiling Millie out the front door to meet Wade on the porch.

His green eyes swept over her, his expression cool. "We're going camping in the hills of West Virginia, not on an African safari."

"What's wrong with my clothes?" Ashby spoke to his back because he'd barely nodded at Millie and Coot before taking her suitcase and turning toward his truck. Millie had directed her to a factory-outlet center in a town some twenty miles away and she'd been pleased to find a Banana Republic store.

Her multipocketed khaki shorts eliminated the need for a purse and the cropped green cotton shirt would provide a cool defense against the heat of the day. As well as being practical, the outfit also showed off her small but curvaceous figure to advantage. She'd made sure of that before she bought it.

"What's wrong with my clothes?" she repeated, when she caught up with Wade.

"You look like a fashion plate." Which was exactly what he'd expected. He'd convinced himself that she'd hate his primitive style of camping and scurry back to her city, leaving him free to feign his broken heart and free to resume his solitary life-style. So why the hell did he feel so angry about it?

As he shoved her suitcase into the back of his truck, Ashby silently congratulated herself on transferring her creams and lotions to plastic containers. "If I'd known I'd be going camping when I left Georgetown," she snapped, eyeing his choice of clothes, "I would have brought my ragbag." Wild horses wouldn't get her to admit she'd bought new clothes for their camping trip.

Wade slammed the back of the truck closed. "Are you insinuating that *my* clothes belong in a ragbag?"

"There are more holes than fabric on your body!"

"Like the view?" With one step he backed her up against the truck, one hand on each side of her, pinning her in place.

"Not bad." Ashby spoke with feigned nonchalance. His cutoffs revealed legs as brown and strong-looking as tree trunks. A split side-seam revealed an equally tanned hip. If he wore any underwear, she was sure it would have to be a G-string not to show. And the slash across his T-shirt provided an enticing glimpse of a hair-roughened bronze chest. Yes, she liked the view. Liked it so much, her knees felt weak and she had to lean back against the truck to support herself.

Wade grinned down at her, careful to hide the answering flare of desire he felt at the look in her eyes. "There are a lot of brambles in the hills. No sense in tearing up perfectly good clothes." With that, he pushed himself away from her and moved around the truck to open the passenger door for her.

Ashby slowly counted to ten, then followed him. The man, she fumed, enjoyed exerting his power over her just a little too much. He would learn that two could play that game. Deliberately, she propped one foot on the dashboard to display the curve of her leg to good advantage, then raised her arms to grip the sides of the truck. Her short shirt rose to reveal several inches of bare flesh.

"Help me up, would you?" she asked, all innocence as she looked over her shoulder at Wade.

He slowly raised his gaze from her legs to her waist and to her face. "Certainly," he agreed mildly, but the gleam in his eyes told her she'd affected him. And his hands lingered on the bare flesh of her waist as he lifted her and set her in the seat.

"Put your seat belt on," he growled and forced himself to pry his fingers from her satiny skin. He walked around to where Millie and Coot waited in front of the truck. "Here's a map," he said, digging into his pocket and handing them a scrap of paper. "If it rains and we're not back in three days, send Jeff out with his four-wheeler. We could get stuck." He glanced back at Ashby. "Although it's more likely that we'll be back early."

Coot cackled. "I doubt it, boy!"

"Have a nice time," Millie said.

Ashby waved goodbye as Wade climbed behind the steering wheel and fastened his seat belt without looking at her. Jamming the keys into the ignition, he gunned the motor, slammed the gears into reverse, backed up, then rammed into first gear and roared away from the house.

"Are you always in such a pleasant mood in the morning?" Despite her disappointment that he hadn't called during the week, Ashby's hopes for the trip had risen to the point that she hadn't packed a single contract so she wouldn't be tempted to ask him to stop if they passed any roadside craft stands. For once, she was willing to devote all her energy to a man, and he was acting like he was sorry he'd ever invited her.

"No." His attention to the road didn't waver.

"Any particular reason you are this morning?" She had to raise her voice over the whine of the tires and the rush of the wind through the open windows as they reached the main highway and Wade accelerated.

He shrugged.

"Why are your tires so loud?"

"Complaining already?" He finally looked at her, but his expression was so hostile, Ashby wished he hadn't.

"No, I asked a simple question!" She held on to her temper by busying herself with rolling up her window. Her hair would be messy enough in the following days; she wanted to at least start the trip looking good.

Wade swerved off the road onto the wide shoulder and braked so suddenly that Ashby rocked against the window.

"If you hate camping and don't want to go, just say so!" he shouted, then noticed her rubbing her forehead where it had hit the glass. "Did I hurt you? Are you all right?" His voice suddenly filled with concern, he unfastened his seat belt and slid across the bench seat to cup her head in his large hands and examine the small red welt.

"Just a bump," Ashby spoke softly, her head bent, not wanting him to see in her eyes how disappointed she felt—or the tears that felt perilously close to the surface. "I've never been camping before, so I don't know how I'll like it. But if you're going to act like a bear the whole time, I'll hate it for sure."

"Oh, hell." He pulled away from her and stared out the windshield. She was right. He was acting like a bear. He turned back to her. "I guess I got out of the wrong side of the bed this morning. I'm sorry."

She smiled wanly, but he saw the vulnerability in her blue eyes and knew the trite excuse wasn't good enough. He leaned forward and pressed his lips to the reddened spot on her forehead, then pulled her close. "I don't want to want you," he confessed. "And I'm mad at myself and taking it out on you." Which was the truth, he realized. The depth of his desire for her scared the hell out of him.

Surprised and touched at his admission, Ashby raised her head and brushed her lips against his. "I feel the same way," she murmured. She felt his mouth curve into a smile.

"And I *hate* your hair that way." He raised his head and ran his fingers through the sleek style, tousling it into wayward curls.

"Why?" Ashby asked, laughing and ineffectually batting his hands away.

He stopped, his grin fading as he studied her. "Because that fancy style makes you look out of my reach."

He was having the same problem reconciling the pull of their attraction with the reality of their differences, she realized. Holding his gaze, she slowly raised her hands to her hair and mussed it. "Well, we can't have that, can we?"

Wade caught his breath at the open invitation in her eyes and in the husky tone of her voice. "No," he agreed and reached out to stroke the sensitive skin of her lips with one finger. "But hold that thought for now." He slid back behind the steering wheel.

"No problem," Ashby murmured, her lips tingling from his touch. That light stroke of his finger had promised exquisite pleasure. She hoped they would reach their destination quickly.

"The tires," Wade said, after he'd pulled back onto the highway, "are loud on pavement because the tread is extra wide and thick for dirt roads. You get used to it, after a while. Music helps." He slipped a cassette into the tape deck and Willie Nelson's voice filled the cab.

"So where are we going?" Ashby asked.

He grinned and reached out to take her hand. "It's a surprise."

Content with the warmth of his hand enfolding hers, Ashby pressed no more. When he turned off the highway onto a dirt road, he had to withdraw his hand to downshift. Ashby gasped as the road grew increasingly rutted and narrowed into little more than tire tracks. She'd opened her window, but now closed it again as the branches of trees whipped toward her.

"Won't we get stuck?" she asked worriedly.

"Not yet," Wade said cheerfully. "We're not even in four-wheel drive. This is highway compared to where we're going."

They reached a stream. No bridge was in sight and Ashby sighed, thinking they'd have to turn around. Wade barely slowed before plowing straight across. Water splashed as high as the windows on both sides of them.

He laughed at her thunderstruck expression. "This is what this baby's for," he explained, lovingly patting the dashboard.

Ashby closed her eyes. The path on the other side of the stream went straight up.

"Time for four-wheel!"

She opened her eyes at the fierce exultation in Wade's voice. He grasped the gearshift with sure confidence and the corners of his mouth curved into a small smile. His excitement was almost as palpable as the roar of the engine as they headed upward.

Rather than give in to the urge to hide her eyes, she watched him as he returned both hands to the wheel and expertly steered the truck as it jounced over rocks and in and out of ruts. Infected by his exhilaration, she laughed and whooped with him as they reached the top of the hill.

"Liked that, did you?" he asked, braking to a stop and turning toward her.

She nodded speechlessly and wondered if her eyes glittered as brightly as his.

"And what about that?" A flick of his hand indicated the view.

She tore her gaze away from Wade's strong features and looked out the windshield. And gasped. She'd known that they had climbed steadily since turning off the highway, but had no idea how high. They were perched on a cliff overlooking a narrow green valley sliced in two by the shimmering sliver of a river. Wildflowers bloomed so profusely along its banks, she could see the purples, yellows and scattering of reds from where she sat.

Trees every imaginable shade of green climbed the slope on the other side of the valley until the darker-hued evergreens thinned near its crest, where stragglers struggled to survive amid the shaley ridges of rock. A seemingly never-ending wave of mountains dipped and peaked in the distance, softened by the lingering drifts of morning mist.

Ashby felt the warmth of Wade's hand enfold her own and turned to him. "Thank you," she whispered huskily, "for sharing this with me."

Wade withdrew his hand to shut off the engine, set the emergency brake and unfasten his seat belt. His movements were slow and deliberate. They had to be to hide the trembling he felt inside. Kay, he couldn't help remembering, had screamed throughout the steep ride, glanced at the scene, pronounced it pretty enough for a calendar, and then reached for the cooler so they could picnic. And that had been that.

But Ashby's eyes were huge and simmering with unfeigned emotion. She truly felt the beauty of this, his favorite place on earth. Had he found his soul mate in this tiny blonde? he wondered. Doubtful. He'd brought her here, first and foremost, to satisfy his nearly uncontrollable craving for her. And secondly, to prove to himself that she was totally wrong for him before he got too deeply involved and risked the hard-won peace he'd made with the life-style forced upon him.

He had a sneaking suspicion that his plan was about to boomerang, but he chose to worry about that later. Right now, he didn't want to think. He wanted to kiss her until they were both senseless.

Ashby watched him as he slid out from under the steering wheel and across the sheepskin-covered bench seat. She read his intention on his face, and her hands met his at the buckle of her seat belt. In her haste, she fumbled with the catch and he gently brushed her hands aside. His fingers, still moving slowly and deliberately, released her, then gathered her up in his arms and into his lap.

At the touch of her lips, Wade felt his control vanish. There was nothing slow or deliberate about the way he plundered her mouth or crushed her against his chest. Nor was there a hint of hesitation in Ashby's wild response.

She'd made her decision: She wanted this man and she wanted him *now*. In one graceful motion, she straddled him, her hips moving in rhythm with the plunging of his tongue within her mouth. His hands slid beneath her shirt and up her bare back, his thumbs massaging the sensitive skin at the sides of her breasts, until they swelled and ached for his touch.

She slipped her hands between them and into the tear in his T-shirt to caress the flat pebbles of his nipples, silently begging him to grant her the same fulfillment. His hips bucked beneath her, but still his fingers teased and tantalized, his thumbs moving forward to trace the curve beneath her breasts, then back again to her sides.

She tore her mouth from his and arched her back, dropping her arms behind her to grasp his hard thighs.

Her shoulders writhed as she thrust her breasts into his hands. Wade's eyes flickered open, but her eyes were closed, her head thrown back, the frantic flutter of her heartbeat pulsing in the blue traceries of the veins in the exposed column of her neck.

Purposely he lowered his hands, then brought them up, outside her shirt. She stilled but didn't open her eyes as he undid first one button, then another. She straightened as he reached the last one and gently, slowly, opened her blouse and slid it off her shoulders.

Her eyes opened, then, to look at him as he looked at her. "Beautiful," he whispered. Her breasts were small, yet full with a natural uplift that scorned the support of a bra. Beneath the heat of his stare, the rosy areolae around their crests puckered as her nipples stiffened, inviting his touch.

Wade bent his head, his hands supporting her back, and she rose to her knees as his lips suckled at first one, then the other taut tip. Ashby moaned, delving her hands into the thickness of his hair and pressing his head closer, intensely aware of the soft sucking at her breast spreading circles of desire wider and wider throughout her body, so out of proportion to the gentle pressure. She wanted more. She wanted to feel his touch everywhere at once.

Her palms cupped his cheeks and raised his head as she dipped her mouth to his and pressed him back against the softness of the sheepskin-covered seat cushion. Again, her fingers dove to the tear in his shirt, this time grasping the ragged edges and ripping the worn cotton away from his body.

She felt rather than heard him gasp, but heedless of anything other than her own need, she pressed her bare softness against the hard, hair-roughened wall of his chest. His hands roamed her back, caressing, massaging, clasping her closer and closer as their bodies moved in steady, escalating rhythm.

The fullness of his arousal strained against the fabric separating them. Feeling its warmth against her, Ashby rode it until she could bear no more, then dropped her hands to his waist. Her need to be one with this man made her heedless of propriety, of modesty, of all restraint, and she yanked at the snap of his pants. Her force pulled the zipper down, freeing him from all constraint.

He groaned deep in his throat, as his hands worked at the buttons of her shorts. No longer capable of his earlier slow deliberation, he fumbled and growled with frustration as she stroked the prize she'd already found.

"Ashby, stop—" He could barely speak. "Help me or…" She kissed him and he could bear no more. With both hands, he jerked at the fly of her shorts and the buttons scattered. She rose to her knees, eager to rid herself of the rest of her clothing. Wade swung her sideways in his lap and her shorts and bikini briefs slipped down her legs to the floor with a sweep of their hands.

He reached, then, into the glove compartment for what had been a last-minute purchase. Ashby needed no explanation when she saw what he held in his hand. She kissed him as he opened the foil packet, then knelt astride him as he slid into the sheath. Their faces level, their breathing ragged, they gazed into one another's eyes, savoring the moment as she hovered over the tip of his arousal.

And then Wade's hands settled on her hips and guided her downward. Ashby closed her eyes and let her head fall back as she reveled in the feel of him filling her. When he moved, slowly at first, she moved with him, quickening the pace as sensation spiraled. Heat seemed to rise in waves, generated from within and without by the friction of their bodies. Sweat slickened the glide of her breasts as they rose and fell against his chest.

And then all feeling centered deep within her as Ashby met him thrust for thrust and she cried out—she knew not what—but Wade heard his name. And her name tore from his lips as he felt her tighten, then convulse around him, catapulting him to an ecstasy that arched his back and lifted him halfway off the seat. Ashby dropped her head to his shoulder and clung harder as his passionate surge sparked another shuddering wave of response in her.

Gradually Wade's tremors faded, and his body relaxed. Although his legs had stiffened and his feet were braced against the floor, he'd supported Ashby's light weight easily, unthinkingly.

As she felt Wade sink back onto the seat, Ashby couldn't move. The most she could do was tuck her feet beneath his thighs. She clung to him, feeling as limp as a rag doll.

"My God," Wade muttered, rubbing her back. "You sure pack a wallop for a little woman!"

Ashby managed a lazy smile as she nuzzled his neck. "If this is camping," she murmured, "I think I'm going to like it."

8

WADE SLID HIS HANDS up Ashby's spine to her neck and curled his fingers into her short hair to tilt her head back. "You ain't seen nothing yet, lady."

"This will be hard to top, you know." Her voice full of throaty challenge, she stretched sinuously.

Wade shook his head. He was in trouble, he realized, as he felt a flare of want revive in his groin. Assuaging his hunger for her had seemed to whet his appetite rather than dull it. He'd thought himself in control of the situation and his emotions, but the little minx wasn't reacting according to plan.

"You tore my shirt," he complained in an effort to put more distance between them. He frowned and glanced down at the tatters still hanging from his shoulders.

"You ruined my shorts."

"Buttons can be sewn back on."

"Your shirt was already torn." Ashby studied his chest. "What is this?" she asked, tracing the pale path of a scar on the tanned flesh with the tip of one finger. She'd been too intent earlier to notice the thin white line running the length of his breastbone beneath the dark mat of curling chest hairs.

"I had to have bypass surgery." He shrugged, his relaxed expression tightening. "Shall we get going?" He lifted her from his lap and set her aside.

"Why?" Ashby made no move to retrieve her clothes.

"Because we can't camp here." Wade pretended to misunderstand her question.

"I mean—" she spoke with forced patience "—why did you have to have bypass surgery?"

"Heart problems, obviously." Wade zipped up his pants and slid behind the steering wheel.

Ashby stared at him, recognizing the off-limits tone of voice. "What kind of heart disease?" she persisted.

"Coronary artery disease." He bent and picked up her clothes and tossed them into her lap. "Put your clothes on." He turned the key in the ignition.

"Explain." Ashby crossed her arms beneath her breasts, her expression as stubborn, Wade thought, as he felt. Why did a woman think that having sex with a man entitled her to know everything about him?

When he shoved the truck in gear and followed the narrow tracks hugging the steep slope without answering, Ashby glumly decided that she'd been right about him. Having a relationship with him was like riding an emotional seesaw. Despite their lovemaking, he'd withdrawn from her, refusing to discuss even his health. She could just imagine trying to discuss emotions. What was left—the weather?

Allowing herself an audible sigh of exasperation, she shrugged into her clothes. There was nothing she could do about fastening her shorts, but she put them on, then rummaged on the floor to find the scattered buttons. She sat up, clutching the buttons in her hand, and stored them in her pockets without a glance at Wade.

Although he kept his attention on the rutted road, he watched her in his peripheral vision. Her movements had been jerky with repressed anger and he swore inwardly. She didn't know what she was asking. His surgery had ended an era in his life and he didn't like to talk about it. But the set of her small chin and the way she angled her head away from him as she looked out over the valley told him that she wasn't likely to forgive and forget.

"Not afraid of heights?" he tried. Kay had kept her head firmly averted from the precipitous drop on her side of the road.

"No." She continued to stare out her window.

"Ever go four-wheeling when you were a kid?"

"No." Her dad's truck could barely be trusted to get them into town, but Ashby chose not to share that tidbit.

Wade's grip on the steering wheel tightened involuntarily. In his book, monosyllabic answers weren't much better than the silent treatment. "Mad at me?" he asked, careful to use a light, teasing tone.

She looked at him, then, without a trace of amusement on her face, replied, "Yes."

"What's so damn fascinating about heart surgery?"

"It is," Ashby answered, barely controlling her own irritation, "a life-threatening situation. A major event in a person's life."

"It happened four years ago!"

"I am sitting two feet away from you. It is not necessary to shout."

Wade clenched his teeth and glared out the windshield. He felt like shouting, dammit! This woman got under his skin and he didn't like it. "It's not something I like to discuss, okay?" he said tightly. "It's over with. I watch my diet, exercise and see a doctor regularly. It's nothing to worry about."

"Is it the reason why you moved to Hickory?"

Wade exhaled explosively. "If you must know, yes!"

"Why are you so angry?"

"Why do you ask so many damned questions?"

"You are," Ashby pointed out, "answering a question with a question. However, I will break the stalemate. I came on this trip to get to know you. If you are interested only in sex, then you have accomplished your goal. You can turn around. Now."

"Now?"

"Yes."

"If I try to turn around, we'll go straight over the cliff. Do you have a death wish?"

"Not for myself."

Wade felt a laugh rising past his anger. "You wouldn't be thinking of me?"

"Absolutely." She stared straight ahead, her expression bland, but her lips twitched. She gave as good as she got, he thought with grudging admiration. No, he wouldn't turn around. He was in charge here and would see this trip through. He'd see how well she liked camping when she got her manicured hands dirty.

They rounded a bend and the narrow track widened into a grassy, tree-lined plateau at the base of a towering cliff of stone. A waterfall tumbled down over the craggy rocks, pooled at the base, then bubbled into a stream that flowed through the small glade and rushed down again over the edge of the mountain.

This, Ashby realized as Wade braked to a stop, was their intended campsite. And it was lovely. "You can turn around here," she said firmly, determined not to base a relationship exclusively on sex—no matter how wonderful it was.

"No." Wade turned off the ignition and pocketed the keys. "If you want to leave, you'll have to walk." He opened his door and climbed down out of the truck.

"What!" Ashby scrambled out her side and slammed the door. She took one step toward Wade, who stood at the back of the camper, and her shorts fell off. He doubled over with laughter.

"You are a natural blonde, aren't you?" he said when he straightened. The wispy lace of her bikini panties hid little.

Ashby glared at him and stepped out of her shorts. If she put them back on, they'd only fall off again, undermining the remaining shreds of her dignity. "Just remember you can look but not touch," she said sweetly.

"Using sex to get your way?" Wade's humor vanished as he spat out the words. He despised women who used sex as a weapon.

"No." Ashby's denial was instantaneous and vehement. "We're not arguing about a diamond necklace or new furniture for the house. We're establishing the basis of a relationship. I told you I wasn't interested in a brief affair. It's too soon to expect a declaration of—" she paused, then forced the word out "—love. But I do expect respect and, and—" She paused again, searching for the right word. "Sharing!"

She nodded, more to herself than to him, pleased with her choice. Yes, it was too soon to talk about love. She wasn't sure about her own feelings yet. As much as the man excited her, he also infuriated her. Maybe, she wondered, Wade had been right when he'd asked if there was a difference between love and war. In his case, anyway, there seemed to be none.

Wade opened the back of his truck with a bang. "Women," he muttered disgustedly as he reached inside the camper.

"Excuse me?" She was beside him now. Wade set the cooler on the ground, feeling quite satisfied with its thud.

"Look," he said, straightening to tower over her, "we're both well over eighteen and, as you said, we're not talking about marriage. When you have everything for your exhibit, you'll go back to Georgetown. Why can't we just have a good time together while you're here?"

Ashby repressed an inner wince at how easily he spoke of her eventual departure. If their relationship progressed as she hoped, they would talk about love . . . and maybe, even marriage. She looked up at him. "Because to me," she said tightly, "a good time involves getting to know another person, and you're not telling me much."

Wade stared down at her. *I don't want to get to know you too well,* he thought. *I might not want you to leave.* He scowled, not liking that idea. Ridiculous. Just because Ashby White was the first woman to interest him since Kay had left didn't mean he was going to fall in love with her. She fascinated and excited him. That was all. After a few days of her, he'd be cured.

"Okay," he decided abruptly. "Coronary artery disease seems to run in families. Fatty deposits form in the arteries and narrow the passageways to the heart. My dad keeled over from a heart attack at fifty-five. No warning, which is not uncommon. I was luckier. I had attacks of angina brought on by physical and mental stress. My heart needed more oxygen and the arteries couldn't supply it."

He paused, his gaze fixed on her face, but Ashby sensed he saw his past rather than her. "I also smoked heavily, loved rich foods and drank a great deal. I exercised, but I chose competitive sports like handball and tennis. I thought I thrived on stress until the angina started and Kay dragged me to a doctor."

He shook his head. "I tried to follow his advice—quit smoking, change my diet and reduce the stress in my life. I took up jogging, but it wasn't long before I was keeping a diary and pushing myself to go farther, faster."

Ashby stood very still, scarcely breathing, afraid that if she stirred, he'd cut short his explanation.

"The angina got worse. The running brought it on so badly, I threw up. I had an attack on the trading floor so painful that I fell and Kay had to protect me from getting trampled." He sighed and ran a hand through his hair. "The doctors decided to operate. They took veins from my leg—" he bent his head and pointed to a small scar on his thigh "—and grafted them to bypass the blockage in my arteries. But they were very clear. The operation would relieve the pain but not cure the disease. I *had* to change my life-style."

"And so you moved to the farm?" Ashby asked softly.

He nodded. "I'd dropped from three packs of cigarettes a day to one and exchanged alcohol for tranquilizers to unwind at night. But I knew that wasn't enough, and while I was in the hospital I realized that I couldn't change my life unless I changed my job. I'd always planned on retiring to Hickory and financially I was already secure, so there was no reason to wait."

"How old were you?"

"I turned thirty-five in the hospital—a great time and place to face forty and review your life."

Ashby nodded. She was quite familiar with the unsettling effect of turning thirty-five and realizing how quickly forty would follow.

"Satisfied?" he asked with more than a hint of sarcasm.

"For now." Her eyes twinkled with humor. There was more she wanted to know. Was he really content with life on a farm after the frenzied life of a stock trader? But she dared not push him any further. Not now.

"Good. I'll set up the campsite, then." He reached inside the truck.

"Anything I can do?"

Wade withdrew his head and shoulders from the camper to look at her with surprise. He'd assumed she'd find a spot to sunbathe and leave him to do all the work—as Kay had done on their picnics. She'd never agreed to camp overnight. "Can you drag the cooler over to the pool and set it in the shallow water? It will help preserve the ice."

"Sure."

Ashby found the makings of sandwiches in the cooler and other containers Wade pulled from the truck and decided to prepare lunch. She'd been too nervous to eat breakfast. When she called him to eat and he didn't answer, she returned to the camper. He appeared from behind some bushes.

"The ladies' room, madam," he said, indicating she precede him through the bushes with a flourish of his hand. Ashby obeyed and saw a roll of toilet paper hung on a branch and a small camp shovel stuck in a pile of dirt next to a hole dug into the ground. She laughed with relief and gratitude. She'd wondered how to handle such arrangements and hadn't wanted to ask. Wade's lighthearted treatment of the situation was thoughtful and touching.

"Plush," she said cheerfully. "Should I tip the chambermaid?"

Wade felt his jaw drop open and quickly clamped it shut. He'd intended to leave her to her own devices, then relented out of guilt. She'd been a good sport about everything from his surliness when he picked her up, through the rough ride and to his nastiness when she asked him about his scar. If anyone was having second thoughts about their relationship, she should be.

He'd still assumed she'd scream in indignation at the primitive facilities, as though she'd expect him to provide a flush toilet as well as hot and cold running water. Assuming anything about this woman, he was learning, proved the old adage that the one making the assumption deserved to be called the term formed by the first three letters of the word.

"Oops, no change." Ashby patted her hips as though looking for her pockets. Wade hadn't pulled her suitcase from the back of the truck so she could find another pair of shorts. Deliberately, she suspected. She'd sensed the heat of his gaze upon her and turned to catch him staring more than once.

"How about a kiss instead of a tip?" she suggested and stood on tiptoe to peck his cheek. Wade turned his head to find her lips, his desire for her surging. Her passion flared to meet his and she strained against him. He ran his hands up and down her sides, over the swell of her hips, in at her tiny waist and up to the small, peaked mounds of her breasts.

Her stomach growled. Loudly. So loudly, Wade couldn't ignore it and he lifted his head. "Sounds like you have another appetite to be satisfied."

Ashby sighed. His kiss had made her forget her hunger until her stomach betrayed her. "I made some sandwiches," she remembered.

With his arm around her shoulders, he turned her toward the blanket spread over the flat-topped rock she'd selected as their table. "Oh, no!" Ashby cried at the sight of a squirrel on the rock. His round cheeks bulging, his jaw working blissfully, he held a small triangle of sandwich in his paws and took another bite as they watched.

"Shoo! Scat!" Ashby darted forward and the squirrel ran up a nearby tree, then chittered at them as if scolding them for interrupting his meal.

"One of the first rules of camping," Wade said, resisting the urge to laugh at Ashby's dismay as she studied the depleted pile of fancy sandwich quarters, "is never leave food unattended."

"Ants," Ashby observed, her expression still crestfallen. "The ants got to them, too." She'd been proud of those sandwiches, having painstakingly cut off the crusts and quartered them into triangles, making them attractive enough to serve at one of her exhibit openings. Luckily she'd left the lids on the jars of pickles and relishes she'd put out.

She looked up at him, searching his face for anger, but saw amusement instead.

"I brought plenty of food, don't look so sad." He gave her a reassuring hug. "Pretty fancy spread for squirrels and ants," he added. "I'm sure they appreciate it, but I don't need it. I like the crusts." He picked up the paper plate of sandwiches and tossed them into the bushes beneath the squirrel's tree. "Here you go, little thief," he called, folding the paper plate and tucking it into a trash bag.

Ashby remained silent as she fetched more turkey from the cooler and bread from the small metal chest that contained food that didn't need ice.

"Something wrong?" Wade asked.

She shook her head, too embarrassed to admit to the disappointment she felt that he didn't appreciate how she'd made their lunch eye-appealing as well as tasty. He seemed quite content to slather his mayonnaise substitute onto the oat bread and slap the turkey on haphazardly. She was unpleasantly reminded of her mental image of him swigging out of a liquor bottle at one of her exhibit openings.

He caught her glance and paused as he was about to take a huge bite. "This isn't one of your social soirées," he snapped, reading her expression as disapproval, "where a man could starve to death trying to fill up on fancy tidbits."

"Did you leave your manners in Chicago?" Ashby retorted as her disappointment transformed into anger. "You could have appreciated the effort I put into lunch rather than make fun of it. Or are you too dense to realize I did it for you and not the squirrel?"

Surprised at her vehemence, Wade cocked an eyebrow as he studied her. Ashby flushed and dropped her gaze to her plate, where she rebelliously cut the crust from her bread. "I enjoy presenting food attractively, as well as preparing it," she mumbled, angry at herself for admitting that she'd wanted to please him.

"You like to cook?" About to bite into his sandwich, Wade paused.

"Yes. Does that surprise you?"

He bit into his sandwich and chewed thoughtfully. "I didn't think you'd have time," he said carefully, after he'd swallowed. He'd heard the defensiveness in her tone.

Ashby arched an eyebrow. "Even career women have to eat."

Wade nodded. "But they can pay someone else to do the cooking."

She shook her head. "Not when they're working two jobs and saving every penny to start a gallery."

"But you could afford to eat out now."

"True, but I find cooking relaxing and rewarding."

"I do, too, now." He paused. "Never seemed to have time when I was in Chicago. Kay and I always ate out or bought take-out food. And, of course, our parties were catered."

Ashby fell silent. She'd wanted to know more about his life in Chicago, but now that he was offering information, she found she didn't want to hear about Kay. They finished their meal in silence—an uncomfortable silence. She caught Wade studying her, but his expression was unreadable.

Had they become intimate too soon? she worried, as they finished eating and she packed away the leftovers. But to have denied the passion that had risen so quickly in the truck would have meant greater unease now. They would have had to dance around their desire for one another until nightfall. Still, the silence felt awkward, as though something had been left unsaid. Needing to escape Wade's nearness, she rose and walked over to the pool to rinse her hands.

Ashby and he might have more in common than he'd thought, Wade realized. He should have followed his first instinct and stayed away. She was adjusting much too well to his favorite pastime of camping. And she enjoyed cooking. Could she also enjoy growing her own food? Understand and come to share the inner peace he felt in his self-sufficient life on the farm?

No. He answered his own question. *Don't fool yourself.* She hadn't denied the fact that she would leave when she'd obtained all the exhibits for her gallery. But that flicker of hope he'd experienced told him something he'd been only dimly aware of—he was lonely.

He didn't like the realization.

9

TO ESCAPE HIS THOUGHTS, Wade lifted his head and stared at Ashby as she bent over the pool. The curve from her small waist, where her cropped top ended, to her bikini briefs was bare to his view, and, he decided, begging for his touch. Moving swiftly, he tackled her.

The mountain water was clear and no deeper than her chin, Ashby realized, as she sank. But it was shockingly cold against her sun-heated skin and even colder compared to the warmth of the large hands on her waist.

"You big bully!" she yelled, when she'd scrambled to her feet and sputtered to the surface. "This means war!" She hit him on his chest, but he pushed her back to arm's length and laughed at her efforts, his green eyes vivid and his teeth white against his tanned face. Determined to exact revenge, she swept back her arms and splashed him. He tossed his head like a playful puppy, then dunked her again.

"Say uncle," he demanded, when she rose to the surface.

"Never!" Ashby took a deep breath and twisted her body as he dipped her below the water a third time. Slipping from his grasp, she dove deeply and swam behind him. Splaying her fingers across his wide shoulders, she lifted herself to push him down. He laughed and flexed his shoulders to toss her off like a troublesome fly, but she wrapped her arms around his neck and her legs around his waist.

He fell backward and they rolled, their weights more equal in the buoyancy of the water. Ashby slung herself around to face him. Wade stood upright, carrying her with him, his strong legs supporting them both as he kissed her.

"You have too many clothes on," he murmured as he raised his head.

"So do you."

Wade released her and they stripped off the offending garments and tossed them onto the shore. He reached for her again, but Ashby slipped away from him.

"Catch me if you can!" she taunted and swam out of reach.

The slick glide of cool water against her bare flesh heightened her anticipation of Wade's warm caresses. The thunder of the waterfall cascading down the rocks above them and crashing into the pool seemed to echo the thunder of her own heart. She'd never desired a man as much as Wade, nor had any other made her feel so desirable.

Swimming directly beneath the waterfall, she let it beat down on her head and shoulders as she turned to face him. He lunged toward her, but she darted to the side and clambered up on the rocks. Raising her arms above her head, she posed, flaunting her nude body.

Wade sucked in his breath at the sight of her pale flesh gleaming wetly against the moss-covered rocks. Her blond hair, plastered against her head, was as short as a boy's, yet her slender curves were all woman.

She was his, he swore fiercely. If not forever, at least for now. He held his arms out to her and she lowered hers to reach toward him as she jumped.

He caught her easily, then slid her body down the length of his as he slowly set her on her feet. She felt his arousal, hard and insistent, as she strained against him, eager for his kiss. She wanted him here and now, in the water. She felt wild and wanton, stripped of clothes and the trappings of modern civilization. Wade was her man and she wanted him with all the primitive force of her instinctual being.

Her hands on his shoulders, she raised herself and wrapped her legs around him as he cupped her buttocks and lifted her. He slid into her smoothly and Ashby let her head fall back, surrendering to the exquisite sensations buffeting her body. Water caressed her breasts in rhythm with Wade's thrusts, and the roar of the waterfall drummed in her ears.

The roar grew louder, as if to match the crescendo of their lovemaking. Not until she felt the misty spray of the waterfall did she realize Wade had moved them closer to the torrent. She opened her eyes and tightened her legs around him.

Their gazes held and they smiled at each other as they paused, suspended on the brink of release. When Ashby pulled herself up to meet his lips, he surged within her at the same time he stepped under the avalanche of water.

Wade felt her body tense and his own stiffened, then he no longer knew whose body was whose as the crash of water against the surface of their skin triggered an inner explosion that tore the strength from his legs.

His knees buckled, but Ashby clung to him and they sank beneath the clear water, tumbling together until they were beached upon the shore. Gasping for air, shaken by the cataclysm that had claimed their bodies, they opened their eyes and smiled, then laughed, sharing the sheer joy of the moment.

Wade gazed down at Ashby, his smile fading as he realized that words of love hovered on the tip of his tongue. Swallowing them, he covered her upturned face with kisses.

A soft smile upon her lips, Ashby basked in the unexpected shower of tenderness, too drained by their earlier storm of sensation to question it. "I could," she murmured, when Wade's attention transferred to her neck, "stay here forever." She felt his lips curve into a smile.

"Might get a little chilly in the winter," he said as he rolled off her and onto his side.

"Realist." A huge yawn ruined the effect of her frown as she snuggled up against him. She tried to smile up at him, but her eyelids felt too heavy to do anything but close.

"Speaking of realism," Wade said worriedly, "we, ah, left our precautions in the truck."

Ashby forced her eyes open to look at him. "It's all right," she assured him softly. "I am protected. Not promiscuous, but careful." She bit her lip, hoping he'd understand.

He studied her face, then nodded slowly. "I haven't been with anyone since Kay." She smiled drowsily and he pressed a kiss against her forehead, then dropped his head down beside hers.

She fit against him as if she belonged there, he mused, as he, too, drifted toward sleep. If only they could freeze this moment in time and stay there forever. . . .

ASHBY WOKE in the glare of the late-afternoon sun, but rather than stir, she stared at Wade. With his face stripped of the mask of consciousness, no trace of cynicism could mar his strong features, nor gleam of devilry escape from behind his closed eyes. Only gentleness remained.

Was this love? she wondered, feeling an unfamiliar swell of emotion rise in her throat. Or simply the aftermath of magnificent lovemaking? She wasn't sure. Yet she knew without a shadow of doubt that in the few affairs she'd had, she'd never felt this close to a man.

Her gallery had always come first. Everything else had paled in significance. And she'd blamed those few lovers for not understanding. They'd understood, all right; understood that they stood a poor second in her life, even when the gallery had been no more than a dream.

But lying here next to Wade, her gallery seemed very far away. She was glad she'd left her contracts and business cards at Millie and Coot's. She felt no need to get up, to hurry off, to search for a new item for her autumn exhibit. Or to beg Wade to sell her his furniture. It was a new and strange feeling. And unsettling.

She lowered her gaze to his chest and moved her fingertip to trace the white scar that betrayed this strong man's physical vulnerability. And suddenly she knew, without a shadow of a doubt, that she loved him. Stubborn, arrogant mule of a man that he was, he could be gentle, tender and considerate. Yes, she loved him. And in a lifetime spent at his side, she knew she'd never, ever tire of him.

His eyes opened and he smiled, seeming to make the transition from sleep to consciousness effortlessly. She smiled back with all the love she felt, but she left the words unspoken. It was too soon to risk exposing those tender feelings; too soon to ask if he felt them, too.

"Was it very frightening?" she asked instead, her voice soft and her finger still on his chest.

He nodded, touched by the earnestness on her face. "I didn't want to die," he confessed. "Forced to confront my mortality, I realized how many things I'd put off and might not have time to do."

"Like what?" Ashby raised herself up on one elbow and propped her head on her hand to better see his face.

Wade linked his hands behind his head and stared up at the sky, formulating his answer. "Big things, like having children and seeing more of Coot and my mother. And little things, like going fishing." He chuckled and glanced at her self-consciously. "Taking time to smell the flowers—that sort of thing."

Ashby spread her fingers across his chest, feeling the strong, steady beat of his heart. "But you didn't have children." Did he still want them? she wondered, and prayed that he did.

He sighed. "Kay was raised in Chicago, had no idea how isolated we'd be. Anna's right, she would have stayed if we'd had a child, but I don't think she would have been happy."

Ashby took a deep breath before asking her next question. "Do you still love her?"

"No." He looked her in the eye and she knew he spoke the truth. She lowered her lashes, not wanting him to see how relieved she felt at his answer.

"A part of me will always love her for making the move," he continued, "and part of me will always hate her for not trying harder to adapt to country life." He sighed and she looked at him again, but he'd returned his gaze to the sky.

"Anna gave her cooking lessons, but Kay couldn't be bothered to figure out the difference between a tea-spoon and a tablespoon. Ask her what the future of a blue-chip stock was, though, and she could reel off the numbers like a computer.

"Living in the country had been a nice dream, but the reality of it bored her. I don't think she thought there was such a thing as a town without sushi bars. She wouldn't try camping and her idea of gardening was arranging flowers in a vase. She tried setting up an in-vestment office, but no one, not even local doctors or lawyers, made enough money to spend on the scale she was used to."

He turned and looked Ashby in the eye. "She stuck it out for two years, I'll grant her that, but we barely spoke to each other for the last one and when we did, it wasn't pleasant. She finally gave me an ultimatum. I could go back to Chicago with her and live in the sub-urbs and be her househusband, or I could stay on the farm alone."

"Why didn't you go?" Ashby knew she risked his wrath by asking the question, but she *had* to know.

"The relationship was on the rocks. I'd changed, and she hadn't. I couldn't imagine myself seeing her off to work every day and staying home doing nothing. That close to the city and with her back trading, sooner or later, I would've returned to work, too. The excite-ment, the challenge...I couldn't have resisted them. Just like a junkie, I would've had to have that fix of adren-aline."

"You couldn't even do it part-time?" Ashby held her breath, knowing his answer would affect how they could reconcile their different life-styles in the future she hoped they'd have together.

He shook his head and she willed her face to remain expressionless as disappointment seared through her. "I don't even handle my own investments." He chuckled. "Kay does. She's married again, has a kid, a big house in the suburbs and her own brokerage firm in the city. She's happy."

"And you?" Ashby asked. "Are you happy?"

About to assure her he was, Wade found he couldn't meet her gaze. "I have been," he said, slipping away from her and rising. "We'd better get dressed or we're going to be very cold when the sun drops down behind that mountain."

Have been? Ashby silently echoed as she looked across the canyon and saw how low the sun sat, seeming to perch atop one high peak. "Brr." She shivered in imagined cold, choosing to let Wade change the subject before she gave herself away and asked him if he could consider living in Washington, D.C. instead of Chicago.

"Go ahead and rinse off while I get us some towels," he said as he picked up their wet clothes and walked away.

He joined her in the pool moments later, then they swam to shore, where he dried her off quite thoroughly. "It's a shame to cover up such a delectable little body," he said, wrapping her in a large towel.

"I thought you didn't like short women," Ashby reminded him as they walked back to the truck.

He grinned. "I seem to be developing a taste for the exception that proves the rule." He nibbled on her bare shoulder for emphasis, then helped her climb up on the bed he'd made in the truck. He'd laid boards across the cabinets built along each side of the camper, then covered them with a foam-rubber mat and sleeping bags zipped together.

"Aren't you going to join me?" she asked with an arch of an eyebrow and a suggestive smile.

"You're going to wear an old man out before his time."

"Who's an old man?" Ashby dropped her towel.

Wade shook his head and reached under the bed to pull out her suitcase. "I am." He set her suitcase on the bed. "And if I don't find some firewood while it's still light, we won't have dinner and I won't have the energy to make love to you again." And he needed time and space away from her.

Ashby laughed and snapped open her suitcase. "With that for an incentive, I'll help you!"

Wade groaned. So far their camping trip had proved how well they could get along rather than how mismatched they were. Bit by bit, his plan was falling apart, wrapping a web of desire tighter and tighter around him. If she liked fishing, he worried, he was a goner.

ASHBY HIKED DOWN the mountain to the river with the agility of a mountain goat the next morning, but after snagging the tree behind her in three successive casts of the fishing rod, she scorned his state-of-the-art reels and lures.

"There's only one way to catch a fish," she declared, then cut a branch off a tree, tied a line around it, added a hook and moved upriver. Too shocked to question her, Wade watched silently, then almost forgot why he was watching as he admired the sway of her bikini-clad bottom.

She stopped and bent over to poke at the moist earth of the riverbank. Wade's mouth dropped open as he saw her lift a wiggling worm and stick it on the hook. In a smooth motion unlike any of her clumsy casts of his fishing rod, she tossed the line out into the river and sat down on a rock, her stick held in both hands and her gaze intent on the water.

Wade threw his head back and laughed at himself. He was caught, he admitted, hook, line and sinker. The woman knew how to fish, however primitive her methods.

Ashby heard him laugh and turned to scowl at him.

"Quiet," she whispered. "You'll scare away the fish!"

He set down his fishing rod and joined her on the rock. "Can you really catch anything with that?"

"Spoken like a little rich boy," she said mockingly. "Of course, I can. My brothers taught me and my father taught them." Wade shook his head in amazement. "You don't believe me?"

"I believe you," he said hastily, recognizing the spark of temper flare in her blue eyes. "I'm just having trouble reconciling the woman sitting on this rock with the woman who drove into Hickory in a Porsche."

Ashby grinned. "What do you have against my car?" Not for the world would she admit that if anyone had told her she'd ever hook a worm again, she would have laughed in his face.

Wade shrugged rather than answer that the Porsche would take her away from him.

"Bet you'd like to drive it," she added slyly. "It's made for hugging these mountain curves."

"On paved roads."

She laughed, remembering the path they'd taken to their campsite. "True!" She felt a tug on the end of her line and went still. Wade saw it at the same time and reached for the stick, but a glare from her made him drop his hand.

When the line went taut and she felt certain the fish was hooked, she stood slowly and backed up a step at a time, freezing momentarily when she thought the pull too strong. Little by little, she brought the fish in close enough to the shore for Wade to catch the line with his hands and haul in the fish.

"A brown trout." Ashby identified the flopping fish triumphantly, as she dropped it into a bucket of water. "Big enough for my lunch. What are you going to eat?"

Wade shook his head as he fetched his fishing pole. "I'd hate to fish with your brothers," he grumbled when he returned.

"Don't worry. One's in Alaska, two are in Texas and one's in Florida. Besides, I'm just as good as they are."

"None of you stayed in Weathersfield?" Wade sat down and cast his line upstream.

"Well, Sue's husband is a West Virginia congressman, but they spend most of the year at their home in Arlington. Wilma teaches at the University of Maryland and Carol is a nurse-practitioner in Baltimore."

"The girls stayed closer to home."

Ashby paused in the act of hooking another worm. "Yeah," she said after a moment, "I guess we did." She tossed her line downstream from his. "All of us get together every few years at someone's house. Grover swears he's going to move if we choose Florida one more time."

Wade grinned. "What about relatives in Weathersfield?"

"The usual aunts, uncles and cousins." She shrugged, and the animation in her voice and on her face faded.

"You don't see them?" Wade hid his astonishment. He didn't have the brothers and sisters she had, but he couldn't imagine his life without the relatives he'd known since childhood.

"I was the youngest in my family and when my parents died, my brothers and sisters had already moved. We sold the house. It wasn't home anymore." Ashby felt defensive. Wade, she believed, could never understand how much she'd wanted to put her poverty-stricken past behind her.

"We could take a drive over there one day if you like."

"Oh, they wouldn't even remember me."

"Sure, they would. They knew you for what? Twenty years?"

"We're never going to catch any more fish if you keep talking."

Wade wasn't ready to drop the subject. "What about your brothers and sisters? Did they turn their backs on their hometown, too?"

Ashby opened her mouth to deny his accusation, then closed it. She had turned her back on her hometown. So what? "No." She jiggled her line irritably.

Wade fell silent, not liking this aspect of Ashby. "Think you're too good for them?"

She stood suddenly and tossed her stick on the ground. "How dare you judge me! You lived in exotic foreign capitals all over the world and came home to Hickory and envied your relatives their walks to school. Well, let me tell you about those walks!"

She took a deep, ragged breath. "I walked in shoes wrapped in plastic and padded with newspapers to keep mud and snow and water from seeping through the holes in their soles. And I wore scratchy, ugly long underwear because my coat was too threadbare to keep me warm! *That's* what I turned my back on!"

Her breath caught in her throat and she felt stinging pressure build behind her eyes. She would not cry, she swore. That part of her life was over. Done with. Finished. She'd never be that cold again. But the pressure built and she saw Wade leap to his feet through a blur. With a choked cry, she turned and stumbled away from him.

Wade caught her easily. Gathering her to his chest, he stroked her hair despite her feeble attempt to push him away. "Let yourself cry," he murmured. He sat down and leaned back against a tree, holding her in his lap.

Ashby didn't have a choice any longer. Safely snuggled in Wade's arms, she let the pain of her past pour out. Her father and his slow death from black lung, her mother worn-out and old before her time, the sneers of more well-to-do schoolmates, the dreams of beauty that had haunted her.

"But there were good times, too," she said, as her painful memories receded. "Fishing like today, family barbecues, cherry picking, taffy pulling. And we were always clean. Ma made sure of that."

She fell silent and Wade hugged her closer to his chest. He wanted to say so much, yet there weren't words to express what he felt. He loved her; he couldn't lie to himself any longer. This little bundle of contradictions—cool sophisticate one moment and barefoot hillbilly the next—had walked away with his heart.

But he wouldn't tell her. To share his feelings with her would be asking her to share his life. And he couldn't do that. Like Kay, she would wither and wilt without the city and the gallery that meant so much to her. And he couldn't share those things with her. A return to the fast pace of the city would lure him back to the world of ambition and competition. And stress.

He knew himself too well. Kay had accused him of extremism, but it was his chest, not hers, that bore the fine line that divided his life into black and white; the line he knew he couldn't cross, not even for love.

Because he loved Ashby, he would hold her now and remember this moment forever. And then he'd let her go.

10

"I HATE TO LEAVE," Ashby said, as she and Wade surveyed their campsite. Other than the ring of stones circling the blackened ash of their nightly fires, no trace of their stay in the green glade by the waterfall remained.

"We're out of food," Wade pointed out rather than admit how much he'd like to stay longer. He had to get back to the farm. He'd arranged for his cousin, Jeff, to look after the chores for three days at most.

"Realist," Ashby grumbled, but she smiled up at him as he opened the passenger door of the truck for her. In the past few days, she'd learned that his mother was right. He hid a soft heart beneath his tough exterior. "There're still fish in the river. I thought you were the self-sufficient type. Can't we live off the land?"

Wade lifted her into the truck, but kept his hands on her waist, his face close to hers. "I left my hunting rifle at home, which is also where my garden is. Why don't you come live off the land with me there?" Nuzzling her cheek, he didn't see her smile slip.

She sat up straighter and pulled back to see his face. He regarded her steadily, his expression guarded. His green eyes reflected neither humor nor entreaty. He'd tossed the ball into her court, she realized. She licked her lips nervously.

"For how long?" Her question hung in the air, seeming to mute the warbling of the birds and the roar of the waterfall.

Forever. "How long can you stay?" he asked aloud.

He wasn't proposing, Ashby thought, and stifled a pang of disappointment. *Rushing things a bit, aren't you?* she scoffed. *He hasn't even told you if he loves you!* But Wade wasn't a man who spoke easily of his feelings. Was this invitation his way of telling her?

Fantastic sex and a few happy days spent in an enchanted glade by a waterfall hardly constituted the basis for a permanent relationship. Living together, day to day, was a far different story. . . .

"Through the middle of August," she said slowly, figuring out her schedule as she talked. A month from now. Her birthday present to herself would be to spend it with Wade. "The gallery is booked through September, but I need at least six weeks to organize and advertise the folk-art exhibit."

"Fine." Wade kissed her on the cheek. "It's settled, then." He closed the door and walked around the truck.

Ashby stared after him. *Just like that?* she fumed. *Discussion closed?* Couldn't he at least say, "Great!" Give her some clue as to how he felt? She'd have a month to figure out this difficult man she loved, though, she consoled herself.

"What will Coot and Millie think?" she asked, as Wade slid behind the steering wheel.

"They'll be pleased as punch."

She ran a hand through her curls, wishing she could straighten them as well as her thoughts. Love seemed to have turned her brain to pea soup. The decision whether or not to live with the man she loved should be simple, but she wanted to know if that love was returned.

"My car can't make it up your hill," she said, thinking of excuses to prolong the discussion.

"The road could use a grading. I'll have it done."

"Promise Samson won't eat me for breakfast?"

Wade chuckled as he turned on the ignition and put the truck in gear. "Knowing you, you'll have him eating out of your hand in the first ten minutes. He looks tough, but he's a marshmallow inside."

"Like father, like son?"

"Are you calling me a marshmallow?"

"If the shoe fits . . ." Ashby bit her lip to keep a smile from spreading across her face at the thought of Wade eating out of her hand.

"You're living dangerously, lady," Wade warned, but he felt curiously lighthearted. His suggestion that she live with him had surprised him almost as much as it had her, but the more he thought about it, the more it seemed a good idea. She'd adapted to camping easily enough; maybe she'd also adapt to life on the farm. *And stay.*

Yeah, right, he silently added. And maybe unicorns live on the farm, too. Who was in charge now? He'd originally wanted no more than a summer romance, and now that she was handing it to him on a silver platter, he wanted more. He should have listened to his instincts and stayed away from her. But it was too late now. He may as well enjoy the summer. If he could survive heart surgery, the loss of his career and the disintegration of his marriage, he could survive the loss of Ashby.

"You're going the wrong way," Ashby said, noticing that he was crossing the meadow rather than returning the way they had come.

"There's more than one way to skin a cat."

He followed tracks that she'd thought were made by other campers selecting a site along the stream. She liked the fact that he adhered to such routes rather than create new ones with no thought for the damage he might cause to the environment.

She looked back at their campsite as they splashed across the bubbling brook. "Almost heaven," she murmured, imprinting the rocky waterfall and lush meadow in her mind. Whatever happened between her and Wade, she would always treasure this memory.

Wade glanced at her. "West Virginia?"

She nodded. "And the past few days. Thank you."

"Yeah, pretty wild and wonderful." His suggestive smile told her he was thinking of their lovemaking. "And I thought you were a prim and proper prima donna."

"Disappointed?"

If she only knew. He'd meant just to please his family and halt their matchmaking, but found himself in love, instead.

Their path around the cliff was narrow, but Ashby stared down over the precipice fearlessly and bade a silent goodbye to the river valley. When the path veered inland and bushes replaced the view, she sighed and turned to look out the windshield. They passed through a tunnel of trees and across a gully, then onto a wide graveled road.

"This is a real road!"

"Yeah, there's a lookout for tourists that way." Wade pointed in the opposite direction. "But our view was even better. This way takes us back to the highway."

"You mean we didn't have to climb that rutted hill we took on the way in?"

"Nope." Wade grinned. "But it was more fun, wasn't it? Especially when we made it to the top."

Ashby eyed him suspiciously, refusing to be diverted by his reminder of the first time they'd made love. "You thought I'd scream in horror and want to turn around."

"Yep." His eyes glinted with humor as he glanced at her. She smiled smugly.

"Fooled you, didn't I?"

"Did you ever," Wade fervently agreed.

BY THE TIME THEY reached Hickory, Ashby could think of little but her first hot bath in days. After a shampoo, a blow-dry and a manicure, she could consider living with Wade more rationally. No, she corrected herself, *stay* with him. It wasn't to be a permanent arrangement. They both knew she'd go back to Georgetown in August. The question was, would he go with her?

"Shall we pick up your things and head on home?" Wade asked, as he pulled to a stop in front of his family's house.

Ashby swallowed nervously. She wished she could make decisions as easily as he did, wished she could be more certain of his feelings. He'd carefully skirted that issue, she realized, despite the intimacy of their lovemaking. For all she knew, she could be going along with his original proposition to have a summer affair.

"What about my car?" She played for time.

"I'll talk to Jeff tonight about grading the road and we'll come get the car as soon as it's done."

"Maybe we should wait . . ." she began, hoping that her reluctance might encourage him to be more persuasive and reveal his feelings, but she saw his mother coming out the front door of the house and fell silent.

"Did you have a nice time?" Millie asked as she joined them by the camper.

"Wonderful," Ashby answered and dismounted from the truck. Wade laughed at the triumphant glance his mother shot him.

"We just stopped by for Ashby's things," he told her. "She's going to stay up at the farm with me."

Millie's mouth dropped open and Wade grinned, pleased that he'd surprised her. He didn't notice that Ashby's mouth, too, had fallen open as he got out of his side of the truck and headed toward the house.

With a quick glance at Millie, half frantic and half apologetic, Ashby hurried after him. "Wade, wait," she called as she entered the house, but his long legs took him up the stairs two at a time and he didn't hear her. Or chose not to? A spark of temper hardened her hesitation into resolve.

"I think we should wait until the road is ready," she said when she caught up with him in her room.

"Why?" Wade opened the closet door and pulled out her suitcases.

Because I'm not sure what you want from me. "Because I may need my car," she said.

He crossed the room and gathered her into his arms. "Today's Thursday. Jeff can grade the road on Saturday. Why sleep alone for the next two nights?" He lowered his head and kissed her.

Why, indeed? Ashby asked herself in what was becoming a familiar haze whenever Wade held her. But she was still troubled when he lifted his head.

"What's the matter?" he asked, knowing he was railroading her and feeling a trace of guilt. "If you're worried about your virtue, it's too late. Coot's store is the hottest gossip spot in town. I doubt there's a soul around that hasn't heard you went camping with me."

Ashby smiled reluctantly. *I want to know if you love me,* she wanted to say, but was afraid to ask. Go for it, her sister had advised. And how else would she find out? He was letting her into his life—and wasn't that the first step toward a commitment?

A weight seemed to lift from her shoulders and her smile brightened. "I'm more worried about a hot bath," she said. "I assume you have hot and cold running water? And a tub, not just a shower?"

Wade repressed a heave of relief, but couldn't resist lifting her into his arms and joyfully spinning her in circles. "Lady, I have a treat for you," he said as he put her down. "I have a hot tub!"

Ashby leaned her head against his broad chest until a wave of dizziness passed, then looked up at him. "Well, what are we waiting for? Let's get packing!"

"Heaven," she murmured barely an hour later as she reveled in the heat of the churning water in Wade's redwood Jacuzzi tub. "There's no 'almost' about it."

Wade chuckled and slid his arm around her shoulders to pull her closer to him. "Liking West Virginia a little better than you used to?"

"Definitely." She rested her head on his shoulder and closed her eyes, too content to say more. After greeting Samson, Wade had carried her across the threshold straight to the bathroom and into the shower. He'd soaped every inch of her body and she'd returned the favor, using her body as a washcloth. Then he'd lowered her into the roiling water of the hot tub and made slow, delicious love to her.

"Glad you moved in?" Wade asked, dropping a kiss on her forehead.

"Hard to say—" Ashby yawned widely "—my suitcases are still in the truck!"

Wade chuckled. "I'll remedy that while you take a nap."

"I'm not tired, just boneless." But she made no objection when he pulled her out of the tub, wrapped her in a huge towel and escorted her to his bedroom. She stared at his bed, speechless for a moment.

"Wade, that's beautiful." Like the chair she'd seen in Coot's store, he'd used saplings stripped of bark for his headboard. The branches all leaned in one direction, as though swaying in the wind.

"A little hard on your back if you want to sit up and read in bed." Wade dismissed her compliment as he tucked her between crisp white sheets. He folded the quilt, a modern mosaic of jewellike golds, reds and browns, down to the foot of the bed.

"Wade—" she wrapped her arms around his neck as he bent to kiss her "—why won't you let me sell your furniture?"

He sighed and rolled his eyes in exasperation, but sat down on the edge of the bed, facing her. "Because, stubborn little lady, I know myself too well.

"I don't do things in half measures." She nodded her vehement agreement and he laughed. "A taste of success and I'd go for the whole pie. I'd start promoting my work in art shows, brochures and magazines. I'd hire helpers and turn this place into a factory. I have this thing about being the best in whatever I do."

"Best doesn't always mean big." Ashby gently traced the line of his jaw. "I wouldn't let you hire out. I'd only sell pieces made by your hands alone."

He pulled away from her and paced beside the bed. "Don't you see? After a while, your gallery wouldn't be enough for me!"

His words snapped Ashby's attention away from his narrow hips and broad shoulders. She stared resolutely at his face as she realized what he was revealing about himself.

"I've done some research and I know there are barely ten people making this stuff these days. And most of them do it in the old heavy Adirondack style with the bark on."

He sat back down next to her and stroked the smooth finish of the wood of his headboard. "I'm sure there's a market for rustic furniture, just like there was in the last century when people first started fleeing the cities and vacationing in the mountains. Pick up any home-decorating magazine today and you see country kitchens and Victorian lace. People still want to escape technology and bring a touch of nature or a bygone era into their homes. But I'm not the one to provide the furniture."

He stared at her, his eyes earnest. "I'd work myself into a heart attack, Ashby. I'm a competitive person, a type A personality, the doctors call it. And my body just won't take the stress I'd put on it."

Ashby propped a pillow against the headboard and leaned back against it as she studied him. She could see the effort his outburst cost him in the rapid rise and fall of his chest. But it was their future he was discussing, whether he knew it or not. And she couldn't agree with him.

"What about the farm?" she asked carefully. "Have you turned that into big business?"

"No, I don't need to. Between the money I made as a trader and what I make from my investments, my income will support me for the rest of my life.

"And, what's more important, I grew up thinking of the farm on a small scale. I don't feel the need to make it the biggest or the best. By the time I bought it, Coot had already sold his cattle, leased the grazing land and limited his crops to his garden. I had so much to learn, I followed his example." Pride touched his face. "I switched to organic methods and rebuilt the chicken coop and smokehouse, though. You ate the first pig I'd raised your first night in Hickory."

"Had you named it?" The dancing lights in Ashby's blue eyes told him her question wasn't serious, but he answered it, anyway.

"Porky, of course." He grimaced. "I learned very quickly where the expression 'eat like a pig' came from!"

Ashby laughed, glad that her small joke had eased the growing tension, but she returned to the point she wanted to make. "And are you going to raise more pigs this year?"

"One or two. I promised Anna and my mother a ham for Thanksgiving, but I don't eat pork." Wade looked at her with confusion, puzzled by her pleased expression.

"But not ten or twelve?" she asked. "You haven't considered selling your hams in grocery stores?"

Wade frowned, recognizing that she was still drawing a parallel between his farm and his furniture to prove that he could keep his hobby on a small scale.

"You should have been a lawyer," he grumbled to avoid the question and tossed the covers over her head.

She peeked out over the top of the sheets. "Blame my brother, Andy, in Texas. He's the lawyer in the family. Sue says we argued from the day I started to talk."

"Poor Andy. How old is he?"

"Forty. And Sue's thirty-eight. She refereed. You should feel sorry for her. Or for me. I was the youngest, so everybody picked on me." She pretended to pout.

"Ha! You were obviously doted on and spoiled rotten."

Ashby sat up and whipped the pillow from behind her back and batted him with it. Wade grabbed the other pillow and both his farm and furniture were forgotten in a free-for-all that ended in lovemaking.

But the conversation haunted Ashby after they got out of bed and she looked at the potpourri of furnishings that decorated his home. Handwoven Indian rugs from the Southwest softened the hardwood floors. Polished wooden statues of African deities perched on the mantel above the fireplace. An ornately carved Swiss cuckoo clock chirped every fifteen minutes. Prints of French Impressionist paintings hung on the walls. A leather-bound collection of Shakespeare's works sat on his bookshelves.

Arizona, Kenya, Switzerland, France and England—he'd been to all those places and more, he admitted under her questioning. But he'd turned his back on them, she realized, for the country life represented by his skirted, overstuffed couch and easy chairs as well as the flagstone-topped coffee and end tables he'd made.

His home was as diverse as he was and, like him, came together to create a fascinating whole. Fascinating but out of reach? Ashby worried sadly. He loved his farm; the pride on his face when he'd talked about it had spoken volumes.

She could share his home, he'd made that clear as he'd emptied a dresser drawer for her lingerie and provided hangers to put her clothes in his walk-in closet. He'd even made space for her toiletries in his bathroom, although he'd teased her about the vast array of colors of nail polish she'd packed.

But he'd never share her home in Georgetown—of that she was becoming more and more certain.

"Hello, anybody in there?" Wade's voice broke into Ashby's musings and she blinked, surprised to see his fingers waggling in front of her face.

"I know a fireplace can be mesmerizing, but I haven't even built the fire yet," he said, brushing a kiss on her cheek as he dropped down beside her.

Ashby summoned a smile, but rose from her seat on the couch, where he'd left her when he went to call his cousin about grading the road. "What did Jeff say?" She sat back down in the easy chair opposite him.

"Saturday's fine. He can use the extra job."

"Is it very expensive?"

He shrugged. It was a long driveway and would cost a bundle, even at the reduced rate Jeff promised. "You're worth it." He grinned. "But I could use a reminder." He patted the empty space on the couch next to him.

"I've been sitting all day," Ashby said, jumping to her feet again and moving toward the door. "I think I'll take a walk." She couldn't stand to look at his living room a moment longer. He'd let his wife go back to the city without him; how could she hope he'd go back to the city for her? What had she gotten herself into? She allowed the screen door to slam behind her as anger pushed aside the ache swelling in her heart.

She struck off blindly. Samson bounded up to her and she patted his head absently, too preoccupied to remember her fear of the big black dog. Apparently taking her gesture as an invitation, Samson lumbered along beside her.

Wade followed her as far as the front porch. "Wait a second," he called. "I'll put some shoes on and come with you." But she didn't look around. Something was bothering her, he realized as he leaned against the railing and debated whether or not to leave her alone. Much of the large farm hadn't been cultivated for years and wildlife had thrived. He'd seen an occasional black bear and even a timber rattler once. But Samson was with her. He'd keep her safe.

He glanced at the horizon and saw the long shadows of evening creeping over the mountains. She'd be smart enough to return before dark. If not, he'd go looking for her. With that decided, he entered the house and headed for the kitchen. He'd fix her a nice dinner, then build a fire in the fireplace. She'd tell him what was on her mind when she was ready.

Ashby wandered aimlessly until she stumbled upon a large, sun-warmed rock atop a hill. She sat down, tucking her feet under her legs Indian-fashion. Samson flopped to the ground beside her and laid his head in her lap.

She stared out at the mountains turning hues of rose and lavender in the last blaze of the setting sun and absently stroked Samson's silky head. "What should I do?" she asked him, but he only sighed contentedly. "I'm in love with the big lout."

The dog raised his head and stared at her. Ashby was sure she saw sympathy in his brown eyes. "And I want to marry him and have his children. But he's in love with his stupid farm!"

She sighed and Samson rolled over to present his stomach for her attention. She took the hint and scratched his belly. "Even if your master loves me, how can I have him and keep my gallery, too? He doesn't seem too keen on returning to the city, you know." The Newfoundland groaned agreeably.

"If I were smart, I'd go back and pack. Get out while the going is good." Her hand stilled as she thought about leaving. Her heart seemed to shrink, then swell with pain at the thought of never seeing Wade again.

Samson batted her arm with his paw, but she ignored him as she raised her knees to her chest, wrapped her arms around her legs and bowed her head. Silently she wrestled with her feelings. Love and Wade, children and family, balanced against her gallery.

"Love is supposed to make you happy!" she finally burst out. Startled, Samson sat up, taller than she was. He nuzzled her neck and she wrapped her arms around him. Taking comfort from his warmth, his tie to Wade, she pressed her face against his shoulder and let her tears fall onto his black fur.

"I want him, I want his children and I want my gallery!" she cried, lifting her head to his. He bent and lapped at her wet cheeks. She laughed shakily and rubbed his ears, then sobered, remembering her sister's reminder that she never set easy goals for herself. Had she chosen an impossible one this time?

"We'll just have to find a compromise, won't we?" she told Samson determinedly. She hadn't found the man she loved only to give him up without a battle. "Washington isn't Chicago. And I'm not Kay. I'm not asking him to go back to trading. And I don't care what he says, he wouldn't have to turn his furniture into big business. I wouldn't let him!

"And I wouldn't ask him to sell the farm, either. It could be our vacation home."

Samson barked excitedly, apparently pleased by her change of mood. "Of course, you could come, too," she assured him. "Washington has lots of parks, we could take you for walks every day." She rose and wiped her hands on her slacks decisively. "I'll call my manager tonight, give her Wade's number and tell her I'll be here through my birthday. I have a whole month to show him that he can't live without me."

Drained of her tears and fears, she felt full of determination and optimism as she headed back in the direction she'd come and Samson lumbered after her. Her step suddenly faltered and the dog passed her as she remembered Wade saying, "I don't do things in half measures." Was the word "compromise" in his vocabulary?

Samson trotted back to her side and nudged her. Lost in thought, she moved forward a few steps and stopped again. Samson whined plaintively, hungry for his dinner. "Okay, okay, I'm going!" she told him, and set off again.

She'd teach that stubborn mule of a man how to compromise, even if she had to hit him over the head with a dictionary!

11

WADE ADHERED TO a country routine, Ashby discovered—early to bed and early to rise. He thought he was doing her a favor by letting her sleep till eight in the morning, her normal rising time. Since he rarely used milk, cream or butter, he didn't keep a milk cow, so she saw no reason for him to get up at dawn.

"Makes a man healthy, wealthy and wise," he argued.

"You're relatively healthy, already wealthy and I seriously question the wise," she countered.

He laughed, but didn't change his routine. While she slept, he collected the eggs from his henhouse, most of which he gave away to relatives, inspected his apple orchards and took Samson for a long walk to check the fences bordering the pastureland he leased to a cattleman.

Then he woke her. Sometimes he joined her in bed and sometimes he brought her coffee or a breakfast tray. Other times he'd gently uncover her, lift her and carry her into the shower or hot tub. Ashby grew to love the sheer unexpectedness of it.

They spent their mornings harvesting the produce from his garden, cleaning house, picking berries or fishing for dinner. Once, Ashby watched him slaughter a chicken, but, despite her upbringing, she'd blanched at the sight of the headless bird still running about the chicken yard and Wade added that chore to his early-morning list.

The afternoons they left free for touring the countryside. Wade drove the Porsche at her insistence. He conceded that the powerful car handled well, hugging mountainous curves with ease, and he tried to accept it as a part of the woman he loved. Alone in the mornings, though, he often looked at it with hatred, knowing it might take her away from him.

Ashby had a list of craft fairs she'd obtained from the Tourism Bureau, but she enjoyed her finds at small roadside stands the most, where the surprise and pleasure of the craftspeople over her interest made her feel like Santa Claus.

Her fairness in dealing with unsophisticated people, Wade noticed, was not limited to his cousin, Anna. She never stinted on her praise or enthusiasm in an effort to negotiate a more lucrative deal. Nor would she allow anyone to take advantage of her.

"I pay for delivery to my customers and I guarantee the return shipping of any unsold items," she told one potter who complained of the cost of shipping his fragile yet heavy items, "but it's your responsibility to get them to me."

"Why?" Wade asked as they drove away.

"The big galleries can afford to have shippers arrive at the craftsman's door, but I can't. This way, the artist shares the risk and the responsibility."

"How much bigger do you want your gallery to get?" Wade was driving the Porsche. He kept his attention on the road, but watched her closely in his peripheral vision.

She smiled, pleased by his interest. The more he learned about her vocation, the more she was sure he'd appreciate, accept . . . and share it. "I've dreamed of Ashby White Galleries in New York and Los Angeles. . . ."

Wade tightened his grip on the steering wheel and damned himself for asking the question. Expanding her gallery into a national operation would mean business loans and negotiations.

"Of course, if I did that, I'd need a good financial adviser," she said, casting him a sideways glance. He stared at the road, not picking up on her hint. "I'm happy with my little gallery, though," she continued. "I don't have to answer to anyone but myself."

"Smart lady," Wade said and Ashby repressed a sigh of disappointment. She'd hoped he'd encourage her to expand and suggest ways and means of doing so. But she found consolation in the fact that, rather than objecting to her numerous shopping trips, he supported her efforts to find the best crafts possible for her folk-art exhibit.

When he volunteered to take her to the Augusta Heritage Arts Workshop in Elkins, where master musicians and craftspeople taught mountain arts and skills at the Davis and Elkins College, she was sure his interest in her gallery was growing. They sat in on classes in lace making, quilting, Appalachian music, white-oak basketry, weaving, pottery, mountain dance and oral history.

"I took all this for granted," Ashby said as they drove home. "All I remember from my childhood was what I didn't have. Even when I got this idea for a folk-art show, I never realized what a cultural heritage I was given." Wade kept silent, realizing that she was thinking aloud.

"Joanna doesn't have anything like this," she continued, referring to her manager and friend. "I always envied her her middle-class suburban upbringing, but now it seems so—" she waved her hand as if trying to grasp the word from the air "—sterile."

Wade reached for her hand as she dropped it into her lap. "Liking West Virginia, are you?" he asked, allowing himself a moment of hope. Would she come to love it, he wondered, enough to choose to stay?

"Very much," she said. "I'm glad that the old traditions and folklore are being preserved. There are too many people like me who have forgotten them."

"Tell me more about Joanna," he prompted, encouraging her to compare their pasts and hoping she'd reach the conclusion that a future in Washington would be as sterile as her friend's childhood. He'd realized that her manager was more than an employee when she'd bought a lace shawl for Millie and a woven one for Joanna at the workshop. The warm rusts, browns and reds of the natural dyes in the latter, she'd said, would complement her manager's red hair.

"She's six feet tall and gorgeous," Ashby told him. "Men fall at her feet. I'm not sure I'll let you meet her."

Enjoying the possessive tone of her voice, Wade managed a smile, but he had no interest in meeting Joanna. He wanted her to stay in Georgetown and Ashby to stay in West Virginia.

A few days later, she found a gift for his grandfather at a country store in the Cass Scenic Railroad State Park, where Wade had taken her to ride the old logging Shay locomotive to the summit of Bald Knob. "Doesn't this look just like Coot?" she asked, holding up a doll.

The doll maker used apples for the dolls' heads, gently shaping cheeks, noses and eye sockets as the fruit dried and withered. Handmade outfits, hats, wigs and even eyeglasses completed the ensembles. The one that reminded Ashby of Coot wore a replica of his favorite denim overalls and included a miniature corncob pipe.

Wade nodded and suppressed his irritation as Ashby went through her routine with the doll maker for her gallery. He'd needed a reprieve from thoughts of her life in Georgetown and had intended this trip strictly for sight-seeing.

"What am I going to do with a doll?" Coot pretended to grumble when she gave it to him, but his lined face beamed with pleasure when Ashby kissed him and told him to put it next to his cash register in the store. She also designed a small card with the doll maker's name and address on it and, at her own expense, had copies printed in case any customers asked about the doll.

"Some businesswoman you are," Wade teased her later. "You're not only creating a competitive market, you're subsidizing it!"

"It's too far away from my gallery to be competitive," Ashby said. They sat on his porch swing, watching the sunset, and she leaned her head against his shoulder. "I wish I had more space, though," she added thoughtfully. "I wouldn't have to be so choosy. A lot of the work I'm passing up is good but not special enough for the gallery." She fell silent, thinking of all the craftspeople she'd met and how much she'd like to help them.

"I know!" She snapped her fingers and sat up. "Why doesn't Coot sell more crafts in his store?"

Wade shrugged, sorry he'd mentioned her business. "Ask him," he said and pulled her back into his arms.

Ashby decided to do just that the following Sunday when they went to Millie and Coot's for dinner. Rather than approach the subject directly, she mentioned their trip to Cass and described the country store there as they sat at the big oval dining-room table. On Sundays, Millie brought out her best linen and china and they ate early in the afternoon. After the table was cleared and the dishes washed, they moved out to the front porch.

Ashby sat next to Coot on the wooden swing, while Millie and Wade settled themselves on the nearby glider. "Your store is just as nice as the one in Cass," she began. "Have you ever considered stocking more crafts and selling by catalog like the general stores in Vermont?"

Coot opened his mouth but, caught up in her idea, Ashby kept talking. "With the right advertising, you wouldn't need a railroad to put Hickory on the map. Tourists would come just to shop at Coot's Country Store."

"West Virginny ain't Vermont," Coot mumbled, his teeth clamped firmly around his pipe. "I remember when we done shipped our maple syrup up there. People paid more for the stuff if'n they thought it was from Vermont."

"That's because the state was one of the first to promote itself," Ashby argued. "West Virginia got on the bandwagon late. Look at all the downhill ski areas springing up or expanding in the past few years. Here in the Potomac Highlands, we've got Canaan Valley, Timberline, Snowshoe and Silver Creek."

"We?" Wade put in skeptically.

Ashby flushed. She hadn't been able to suppress her surprise at the development he'd shown her on their sight-seeing trips. She'd been especially impressed with the new indoor pool and fitness center at the oldest resort, Canaan Valley. Reverting to his former cynicism, Wade had sneered that she'd thought the state had remained frozen in time since she'd left.

She'd kept silent then, as she did now, unable to deny the truth of his statements. She should have guessed that the state would turn to tourism to support its economy as coal mining waned, but she hadn't. The picture in her mind, drawn in childhood, had remained fixed.

"She is a West Virginian," Millie reminded Wade.

"Yeah, right." Wade crossed his arms over his chest and stretched his legs in front of him, halting Millie's gentle swaying of the glider. "She's such a West Virginian, she hasn't been to see her relatives in Weathersfield for fifteen years. And doesn't intend to. Ever."

Ashby gasped, remembering the last time he'd accused her of turning her back on her family. She couldn't believe that this was the same man who had held her when she'd cried over her childhood. "And I explained why," she said unsteadily.

Wade saw the reproach shimmering in her luminous blue eyes and looked away. He'd wanted to hurt her, he realized; wanted to diminish her in his family's eyes. Because he resented her art gallery. Everything she did came down to that.

"Ain't nuthin' more important than family," Coot said, forgetting to puff on his pipe as he frowned at Ashby.

"I'm sure she has her reasons and Wade knows them," Millie said gently. "He's just being his nasty self, and I think I know why." She leaned over and whispered in Wade's ear, "Ain't love grand, son?" Wade scowled.

A smug smile still on her lips, Millie turned to her father and shifted the subject back to his store. "I think Ashby is on to something. Anna isn't the only one still making beautiful quilts and such, right here in Hickory and Clairmont. We'd not only help people like her, but think of the restaurants and inns that could use the tourist business."

"People need a place to buy food, too," Coot said. The wrinkles on his lined face seemed to deepen with thought as he relit his pipe and sent a small cloud of aromatic smoke in Ashby's direction.

"With some rearranging you could do both," Ashby said. "And you could expand as your business grew." She cast an anxious glance at Wade, longing for his support, but he sat stone-faced and silent, not looking at her.

"Don't know as I'd know what I was doing, neither," Coot added. "Hard to teach an old dog new tricks."

"I'd help you," Ashby said eagerly. "We'd start by distributing brochures at my gallery. My folk-art exhibit would pique people's interest and the brochure would tell them where they could go to find similar items."

"How am I supposed to know what them city folk would like?" Coot said, tapping the dead ash from his pipe and refilling it.

"I could make arrangements for your store at the same time I'm making them for my exhibit," Ashby offered. "And Millie has a good eye. I can tell that by looking at how she's decorated the house." Millie smiled at the compliment and Ashby allowed herself a thrill of hope.

"And when your exhibit was over," Wade said harshly, "we'd be on our own."

"Not if you married her!" Coot crowed.

Wade jumped to his feet. "I'm going for a walk." Ashby stared at his broad back as he stalked away.

Millie rose and joined them on the swing. Ashby made room for her without thinking, her gaze still fixed on Wade.

"You love him, don't you?" the older woman asked her softly.

Reluctantly, Ashby pulled her gaze away from Wade. "Yes," she answered honestly and wished the admission made her feel happy rather than sad.

"And he loves you." Millie hugged her. "Just give him time to admit it."

Ashby accepted the warm embrace gratefully, but she cried inwardly. She needed to hear those words from Wade. August had arrived and time was running out.

WADE BARELY SPOKE to her when he returned and drove them back to his farm. Ashby felt she deserved an apology and also remained mute. When they crawled into the wide bed, each kept to the outer edges. But Wade woke in the night and reached for her.

They made silent yet tender love and when it was over, Wade held her gently. "I'm sorry," he said, brushing her forehead with his lips. "I shouldn't have said that about your relatives."

Ashby wanted to ask why he'd done it, but deemed it wiser to accept the apology she sensed was so difficult for him to make. "You're forgiven," she murmured, snuggling closer and kissing his shoulder.

"You said your mother's maiden name was Ashby, didn't you?" he asked.

She made an affirmative noise in her throat, then mumbled a drowsy, "Why?"

"No reason. Go to sleep." He ran his fingers through her short hair and, soothed by his stroking, she drifted off to sleep. Wade lay awake, formulating a plan to forge a new bond to tie Ashby to West Virginia—and him.

He rose as the first rosy hues of dawn brightened the sky and called Information. He tucked the telephone numbers he obtained in his wallet for later use, then went about his chores.

When Ashby woke and glanced at the clock, she was startled to see that it read almost ten. Why hadn't Wade come to her? Had she dreamed his apology? she wondered, as she rose and showered and dressed.

He still hadn't appeared when she was finished, and she went looking for him. First, she checked the garden. He wasn't there, but she noticed that the door to the barn was open. She'd been allowed admittance once and learned that she'd been right when she guessed it was his workshop. He made most of his furniture in the winter, he'd told her, when the cold and snow limited outdoor activities.

"Hello?" she called, hesitantly poking her head inside the door. "Anybody home?"

Wade turned, his silhouette outlined by the light streaming through the huge window he'd installed in the eastern wall of the barn. Samson rose from his spot at Wade's feet and, tail wagging, ambled over to greet her.

"You're up early," Wade said, putting down a branch and coming forward to wrap her in a bear hug. Samson rose on his hind legs and propped his front paws on his master's arm, clearly wanting to be included. Ashby laughed and put an arm around the dog.

"Early? It's ten o'clock!" She smiled up at Wade, reassured by his greeting that she hadn't dreamed his apology.

He glanced at the wall clock by the door as he released her and Samson dropped down to the floor. "So it is. I didn't notice. Come see what I'm making." He took her by the hand and led her to his worktable. She saw a tree trunk, split in a V shape, each side eight feet high, with most of its bark already peeled.

"I noticed it this morning when Samson and I were checking the fences," Wade explained. "Saplings rarely divide in such equal pieces. One side usually claims the most water and nutrients and grows thicker than the other."

He paused. "I thought it would make a perfect quilt rack." He lifted the piece and set it on the floor with the point toward the ceiling. "I'll put four rungs across it," he explained. "You could use it for some of Anna's quilts in your exhibit, if you'd like."

Ashby sucked in her breath. "I'd love to!" Her eyes shone with pleasure. Was the rack a token of the love he couldn't bring himself to admit? Was he thinking of a future with her?

"Do you want it back after the exhibit?" she asked cautiously.

"Keep it or sell it, whatever." Wade shrugged. He'd seen the sapling and decided to make the rack for her as a peace offering. He'd been wrong to attack her as he had yesterday. Her gallery was a part of her and he had to accept that. And if it took her away from him, he had to accept that, too. There was no sense in spoiling what little time they had left with useless arguments.

Ashby hugged him, her smile radiant. She wouldn't press for more, she decided, certain that the quilt rack was Wade's first step toward exhibiting his work in her gallery, the first step toward a compromise that would allow them to spend the rest of their lives together. He was a proud man and if she pushed too hard, he might dig in his heels and turn stubborn. She would wait for more.

In the ensuing days, Ashby followed the progress of her quilt rack with keen interest. Wade peeled off most of the bark by hand with a metal scraper. He then used an electric sander, the only power tool he allowed himself. To drill holes and carve the fittings, he used hand tools: a brace and bit, chisel, file and dovetail saw.

The sanding, he explained, was the most tedious part of the job and he simply didn't have the patience to do it manually. But once the piece was assembled with dry rungs crossing the inner V and joining the two sides of the green sapling, Ashby saw how patient Wade could be.

His big hands caressed the wood as lovingly as he caressed her body. He applied coat after coat of linseed oil and mineral spirits. He waited for each coat to dry before adding the next, then did the same with five layers of paste wax. The process, he explained, protected the wood and highlighted the grain.

Ashby watched his big hands at work and knew he loved what he was doing. He took pride in the smallest details. She could tell by the satisfaction on his face as he trimmed the knot at the end of one leg so that it looked like the carved ornamental foot of a Queen Anne cabriole. He seemed to forget her presence as he shaved a bit of wood at a time, then stood the rack on the floor to check its balance.

"It's so odd," she said one day as she watched him, "that you could have been such a high-powered stock trader and now do this."

He turned and studied her. She sat Indian-fashion atop a tall stool, her small feet tucked beneath her legs. She'd propped one elbow on a knee and rested her chin on her hand. Her hair had grown and she'd stopped trying to tame her curls. The softer style made her look young and vulnerable and sexy all at the same time.

"It's a kind of therapy," he explained, choosing a clean rag to wipe the wax from his hands. "Just as important as watching my diet and exercising. It's relaxing, yet gives me a sense of accomplishment, too." He grinned as he crossed the room to her. "Kind of like making love to you."

He pulled her over to a pile of fresh hay he'd grown and recently harvested to use as a winter mulch in his vegetable garden and flower beds and lowered her onto it.

They got to the garden late that day. Ashby picked the green beans lower on their poles, while Wade picked from the taller vines. When they returned to the house, she eyed the mountain of legumes they'd dumped into the sink for washing.

"I can't eat another bean," she declared, "in any way, shape or form. Let's freeze or can them all." Wade strictly adhered to a low-cholesterol diet of vegetables and white meat, she'd discovered and had quickly adapted herself to it. She enjoyed the exotic dishes he prepared when it was his turn to cook. Chinese was his specialty.

Wade chuckled. "We can pawn some off on Mom and Coot, I suppose. I'm not sure how much more I should put up for the winter. Do you think I'll be feeding one or two?"

The colander of green beans Ashby had been rinsing in the sink slipped from her suddenly nerveless fingers. Feeling as if she were moving in slow motion, she watched her hand reach toward the faucet and turn the water off. Then she turned to the stove, where Wade was putting a pot of water on to boil.

No glint of humor shimmered in his emerald eyes as he leaned back against the stove and returned her steady gaze. He wasn't teasing her, yet neither did his face reveal hope or fear. For all she could read of his expression, he could have asked her if she thought it would rain.

"Is that an invitation to stay?" she asked hesitantly.

"Do you want it to be?" His tone was as neutral as his face.

The word *yes* rose to Ashby's lips, but she bit it back. "Are you asking me to stay?" She rephrased her question, wanting to be sure she understood him.

Wade crossed his arms against his chest and studied her silently. Her hesitation had given him his answer. She wasn't willing to give up her gallery to marry him. He couldn't fight something she'd worked so hard to attain.

Ashby reminded herself to breathe as she waited for him to speak. The silence felt heavy with things left unsaid. Did he love her? Did he want her to stay? Why was he leaving the decision up to her? Only the soft sound of Samson's panting as he lay at her feet disturbed the quiet.

"No, I can't do that," Wade said and turned back to the stove.

"Why?" The word tore from Ashby's throat.

Wade swung around and crossed the distance between them in two long strides. Gathering her up in his arms, he sat down at the table and held her close to his chest. "Because, lovely lady, I love you."

Ashby raised her head. A warm flood of joy seemed to wash over her. "And I love you."

Wade hugged her fiercely, glad, despite his misgivings, that his feelings were returned. Then he lifted her face to his. "But we're both old enough to have learned that love can't conquer the distance between West Virginia and Georgetown."

Ashby stared up at him, her happiness dimming at the sight of the sadness in his eyes. "Love will find a way," she assured him, her spirits rising again, certain that their feelings for one another would lead him further toward compromise. "We're two mature, reasonable adults. We'll find a way to be together."

Before he could ask how, she kissed him. Now was not the time to discuss who would give up what, she told herself. Now, all she wanted was to bask in the knowledge that he loved her.

12

As THE HOT EARLY DAYS of August melted into one another, Ashby and Wade kept to themselves, rarely straying from the farm. Ashby had finished acquiring for the craft exhibit and was free to devote all her time to Wade. Rather than driving through the countryside in the afternoons, they took long walks on the farm picking late blueberries and searching for the ripening blackberries or simply admiring the mountainous vistas.

The future remained a blank, a shadow lurking on the fringe of her happiness, but Ashby refused to worry about it. Wade's every glance and gesture assured her that his love was as deep as hers. Conversations started, then seemed to stop as their eyes met in a gaze that suspended time.

Certain that he, too, was planning a future together, she prepared herself to make her own compromises. If his stand against returning to the business world was as irreversible as it appeared to be, she'd relinquish the idea of expanding her gallery with him as her financial adviser. Instead, she'd keep the gallery small and turn more responsibility over to Joanna, which would allow them to spend less time in Georgetown and more time on the farm.

When he became increasingly secretive as her birthday neared she guessed he would share his plans with her then. He'd finished her quilt rack, but still hadn't completed all his morning chores by the time she awoke and he began locking the barn. She also caught him in several hushed telephone conversations that abruptly changed tenor when she walked into the room. And once, he called her to the phone to speak to her sister long after it had rung.

"Just getting to know the man that hooked my baby sister," Sue had explained, but Ashby's suspicions mounted. Wade had promised her a memorable birthday, but would say nothing more.

Her hopes swung like a pendulum: He was going to propose and had asked her sister her ring size.... He'd decided to sell his furniture and was secretly building an inventory.... He was going to break off with her and had invited her sister to visit under false pretenses so she'd be there to comfort her....

She knew she couldn't delay her return to Georgetown much longer. Calls from Joanna grew more frequent as the items she'd selected for the exhibit were delivered. "Soon," she promised Joanna repeatedly. "I'll be there soon."

Wild horses couldn't drag her away from West Virginia before her birthday. She found it ironic that this, her thirty-fifth, the one that had filled her with such restlessness, now held the key to her future happiness. But her spirits dipped as a steady rain set in two days before her birthday. A bad omen, she feared.

"Cabin fever already?" Wade asked, noticing her listlessness as she picked at her grapefruit at breakfast the second morning. They'd stayed in the previous day. Wade had gone into town to rent movies, while Ashby baked oatmeal cookies. When he'd returned, she'd made hot chocolate while he built a fire in the stone fireplace, and they'd snuggled on the couch together.

She shook her head. "I had a lovely time yesterday. It's just . . ." She gazed out the window at the gray day. "I don't want it to rain on my birthday."

"What's the matter, little girl?" Wade asked, moving around the table and kneeling by her side. He wrapped his arms around her waist. "Afraid it's going to rain on your parade?"

Ashby nodded gravely. Silly as it was, she did feel like a little girl.

"Don't worry," he said reassuringly. "Neither rain nor snow nor sleet shall slow your descent into middle age!" He grinned, dropping his pretense of sympathy.

"Oh, thanks! That makes me feel *much* better." She balled her hand into a fist and cuffed him lightly on the cheek. "Of course, how could I expect an old man of thirty-nine to understand?"

"Old man!" Wade's eyes widened with comic outrage. "I'll have you know that *Newsweek* reports that the forties are now considered the last stage of youth."

Ashby tapped her chin as she pretended to ponder his point. "Well," she said after a moment, "that's probably true of me. After all, a woman doesn't hit her prime till forty. You poor men hit it at about nineteen. That makes you twenty years too old for me!"

"Oh, yeah?" Wade rose to her bait. "We'll see about that!"

They didn't watch movies that day and they didn't bake cookies. They did build a fire, a roaring fire. But the heat of those flames couldn't compete with the heat of their lovemaking on the soft pile of the sheepskin rug in front of the fireplace.

The sky cleared just before sunset and a rainbow arced across the sky. Stark naked, Ashby ran out to the front porch and crowed with delight. Wade followed her more slowly and found her clapping her hands and hopping from foot to foot. She hugged him fiercely, certain that the rainbow was a portent of good things to come.

She woke before Wade the next morning. Cautiously edging out of bed, she shivered in the chill of the predawn air and confiscated his heavy flannel robe. When Samson raised his head and peered at her in the darkness, she raised a finger to her lips and whispered, "Shh." He yawned and rose, then shook himself and she froze, afraid the jangle of the tags on his collar would waken Wade.

It didn't. Inching out a dresser drawer, she selected a pair of Wade's heavy socks and carried them to the kitchen. Samson lumbered after her. As quietly as she could, she filled the coffee maker and hit the brew button, then donned the socks and quietly opened the kitchen door to the back porch.

She curled up in a rocking chair, wrapping the voluminous folds of Wade's robe around her. Samson settled beside her, laid his big head on his paws and resumed his interrupted sleep. She would wake Wade when the first rosy hue of the rising sun lit the sky. She wanted him with her as she greeted the dawn of her birthday, the day he would ask her to be his wife and share his plans for their future. How could a rainbow be wrong?

"There you are!" Wade's voice at the door behind her startled her. "And my robe, too, I see."

"I was going to wake you." She smiled up at him, loving him. He'd donned a ragged green sweatshirt and jeans, and his black hair was still tousled from his sleep. He looked wonderful.

"After you ransacked the house for a present?" he asked, his grin teasing. "You're worse than a kid on Christmas morning!"

Ashby rose as he pushed through the screen door. Standing on tiptoe, she kissed him. "You're all the present I want."

Wade bent and hid his face in her hair and held her for a long, silent moment. "Well, you've got me," he said gruffly, when he could trust his voice. "I'm your slave for today. What would you like for breakfast?"

"French toast smothered in maple syrup," Ashby replied, repressing a sigh of disappointment. She'd handed him an opening for a proposal on a silver platter and he hadn't taken it. He knew she had a romantic streak, though, she reminded herself. Maybe he was going to wait and ask her over dinner in an elegant restaurant. Or take her for a moonlit stroll. "No healthy stuff like fruit or oatmeal!"

Wade laughed. "Tired of my diet?"

She shook her head. "No, but today is total indulgence for me. If you ask nicely, I might even let you have a bite."

"Big of you, little one." He lifted her, then sat down in the rocking chair she'd vacated, holding her in his lap. "Let's watch the dawn first, okay?"

"My thought exactly," she agreed, and rested her head on his shoulder.

Wade told her to dress and prepare to leave after breakfast. "Wear something nice but not too formal," he advised. That ruled out camping, Ashby mused as she studied her wardrobe, but left the possibility of a romantic dinner. But what was he planning for the intervening hours?

Her mystification deepened when he slipped into khaki-colored slacks rather than his usual jeans, a teal blue short-sleeved dress shirt and slung a corduroy jacket over his shoulder.

Dressed, he turned to her. "If you don't put something on over that lingerie, we're going to be late."

Ashby smiled invitingly, but he shook his head and made for the door. "Ten minutes or I'll haul you out to the car in what you have on." He closed the door behind him.

Ashby studied her limited wardrobe, wishing she had something new to wear. The bedroom door opened and Wade walked in, carrying a dress box wrapped in gaily colored paper and topped with a big yellow bow. "Happy Birthday," he said, a grin stretching across his tanned face.

Ashby pounced on him and he led her to the bed. "Open it," he said, seating her and placing the box in her lap. Obediently, she tore the paper off and tossed it on the floor. She took a deep breath before opening the lid. Would it be like a Chinese puzzle—a series of boxes opening to smaller and smaller ones? To a ring box? she prayed.

No. White tissue stared up at her. Gently, she folded back the paper and found a white dress trimmed in cotton lace and hand-embroidered pastel flowers. "It's lovely," she said, keeping her gaze on the dress as she swallowed her disappointment. "Thank you."

"Thank Anna. She made it. She thought you might like something special to wear."

Ashby raised her head. Relieved that the dress wasn't his gift to her, she smiled. "I didn't expect a present from Anna," she said, standing and slipping the dress over her head.

"She wanted to do it. You look gorgeous."

Ashby looked into his eyes and felt beautiful even before she turned to the full-length mirror on the closet door. The lace dropped from an off-the-shoulder neckline and matching lace fell from the hem. The pastel flowers formed a border where lace met cotton.

The straps of her silk camisole showed, so she slipped out of it and tossed it playfully at Wade, who stifled a groan and glanced at his watch.

The dress, Ashby thought as she turned back to the mirror, made her look—and feel—deliciously feminine. Perfect for a romantic proposal.

"Not bad for a thirty-five-year-old broad," Wade said as he headed for the door again. If he touched her, he knew they'd be late. He was beginning to regret that he'd chosen to share her today. He heard the shoe she tossed after him hit the door.

He had no idea how she'd react to his surprise. He only knew what he hoped to gain—the re-creation of another tie to West Virginia and, consequently, to him.

When Ashby joined him, Wade headed to his truck, while she aimed for her Porsche. "My surprise and my choice of vehicle," he told her. He didn't want any reminders of Georgetown with them today.

A picnic in an out-of-the-way, beautiful spot, Ashby thought, as she obediently moved to the truck. Her engagement ring was probably hidden in a basket in the back.

Wrong again, she realized, as Wade drove straight to Hickory. She laughed when she saw all the cars and trucks parked along the lane in front of his family's house. "Did you invite the whole town to my surprise birthday party?" she guessed. Maybe he wanted his entire extended family present for the announcement of their engagement, she prayed, then crossed her fingers for good measure.

"The whole state," Wade agreed and tooted his horn to announce their arrival as he pulled into the space left for them in the driveway in front of the garage.

Millie met them inside the front door. "Happy Birthday," she said and hugged Ashby. "Coot and the family are out back." She led her to the back door, which Wade opened.

Ashby stepped out onto the porch and blinked, unable to take in everything at once. The green lawn was filled with brightly colored canopies shading tables of food, a huge banner wishing her a happy thirty-fifth hung from two posts and a mob of people were standing at the bottom of the steps and singing "Happy Birthday" to her.

Her vision blurred as she recognized faces in the crowd. They were the faces of her family, as well as Wade's. Her sister, Sue, stood in the middle, her husband by her side and her children lined up in front of her. Her sister, Carol, and her family were on Sue's right. Her brothers from Texas, Andy and Frank, stood together on the other side of Sue, with Grover, from Florida. Having farther to come, her brothers must have left their families at home, she guessed.

The birthday song ended and Sue surged up the steps when Ashby remained frozen in place. "Well, kiss the guy," Sue commanded. "This is all his idea!"

Ashby turned to Wade, still speechless. He grinned and held his arms out to her. She moved and he kissed her very thoroughly amid thunderous applause. And then they were separated as the crowd enveloped them.

"Lucky your birthday fell on a Saturday," Andy told her. Almost as tall as Wade, but of slighter build, he ducked his head down to kiss her cheek.

"Couldn't have made it otherwise," Frank chimed in. Lighter-haired and shorter than Andy, he hugged her, then winced in mock pain as Ashby playfully patted his developing paunch.

"Couldn't take enough time off for the family to come," Grover explained. "They send you the best." His tan was almost as dark as Wade's, although he was as fair as Ashby.

"Bill was really sorry he couldn't make it," Carol said, referring to their brother in Alaska. "He's going to call today."

She was the oldest, Wade guessed; her hair was as gray as his mother's. He counted heads. "Isn't there someone besides Bill missing?" he asked.

"Wilma's on sabbatical in France this year," Sue answered. "She's a professor at—"

"The University of Maryland," Wade finished.

"Very good!" Sue's blue eyes flashed as brilliantly as her smile, Wade saw. The tallest and darkest-haired of the women, she wore a vivid red dress and allowed her brown curls to tumble down to her shoulders.

"If you can keep all of us straight, we'll give you a grade-A stamp of approval," she added. Wade grinned and rose to her challenge, pointing to each one and ticking off their names, glad he'd paid attention when Ashby had described them. Sue thumped him on the back as the promised stamp of approval, then turned and beckoned to a woman shorter than Ashby.

"You remember this lady, don't you?" she said. Fifteen years had lined that familiar face, but Ashby recognized it immediately. Wade and Sue had invited more than her immediate family.

"Aunt Tootsie! Well, at least I grew as tall as you!"

"And got yourself a man as big as my Elwood," her aunt said with a smile at Wade.

"You was always a pretty little thing," Elwood said, "and you still are."

"You used to call me Cherry Popsicle," Ashby remembered. "Where's Nancy?" Their daughter was two years older than she and they'd been close friends. Nancy stepped forward, her features so like Sue's that they could still be mistaken for the twins they'd pretended to be in their childhood.

Conversations started and stopped as names and faces clicked in Ashby's mind. Her Uncle Galen, tall and thin. His wife, Florena, her face round and gentle. Her Aunt Marguerite, whose height she'd always envied, was now shortened by age and the effects of osteoporosis. Her husband, Clyde, was still quick with the wit that had always made her laugh.

Ashby teasingly refused to believe her Aunt Gerry's gray hair was natural. It had shifted from black to blond to red so often while she was growing up, she'd never known what the true color was. Her Aunts Kathleen and Betty, she swore, were as petite and trim as ever.

Many of her uncles had passed away, like her father, from black lung. But she remembered them vividly. Floyd, Phrae, Jim, Cletus. And many of her cousins had, like her, moved away, but still lived close enough that they'd come back for her party. Chuck, Jerelyn, Twila, Stogie, Dottie, Jack, Donna... They'd all grown up, but they joked about the pranks they'd played on one another as though it had been yesterday.

"Remember when Nancy switched Ashby's chocolate pudding for cold gravy and Ashby took a big bite?"

"And Ashby got her back by putting vinegar in her water glass?"

Their children looked askance upon them as they roared with laughter, obviously loath to believe that their parents ever could have been that young. And through it all, Ashby saw the love and interest on Wade's smiling face. No matter that the stories had nothing to do with him, he laughed as heartily as the rest. His relatives had been invited, too, and they mixed and mingled—one big happy family.

"Reminds me of a weddin'," Coot said as he joined them at a table. "All's we need is a preacher. Bet we could get old Jenkins over here."

"Need more notice," Andy said. "Bill and Wilma would never forgive the pipsqueak for getting married without all of us present."

Ashby stole a glance at Wade. He was smiling, but she couldn't tell how he felt about the talk of their marriage.

"What's Bill do in Alaska?" he asked, changing the subject, to Ashby's disappointment.

"Runs a hunting and fishing camp out in the middle of nowhere," Frank answered. "People come from all over the world and pay him to do what he loves best." He shook his head and patted his belly. "Me, I sit in the office all day writing legal briefs for corporations and eat too much at business lunches."

"Come on down to Florida and I'll work that fat off you," Grover said.

"Another tough life," Frank explained for Wade. "He runs a sailboat-charter business."

"You and Ashby visit and I'll take you deep-sea fishing," Grover offered.

"I fished with her once," Wade said and shook his head dolefully. "I'm not sure my ego can take it again."

"Remembered what we taught you?" Andy asked.

Ashby nodded. "I gave credit where credit was due."

"Remember the time when we convinced her we'd brought her to the fishing hole to use her for bait?" Her cousin Chuck joined the conversation.

"She climbed a tree and wouldn't come down until you guys came and got me," Sue remembered.

"Told you everybody picked on me," Ashby said to Wade.

"Poor baby." He hugged her, but his eyes reflected more amusement than sympathy.

"She gave as good as she got," Frank swore. "I remember the time when . . ."

Story followed story as the day wore on. Ashby felt her eyes grow misty when the conversation turned to her parents. She saw their features when she looked into the faces of her aunts and uncles.

"Thank you," she whispered to Wade as they moved together from one group of people to another. "Thank you for giving me back my past." In his characteristically high-handed fashion, he had disregarded her reluctance to see her hometown relatives, but she couldn't resent him for it.

"Happy?" he asked and she nodded vehemently. No one had forgotten her any more than she had forgotten them. Nor did she feel pain at the memories stirred by the familiar faces. Her fears had been groundless.

"That's thanks enough." He winked lecherously. "Until later, anyway."

There was only one thing that would make her happier, Ashby thought, as another group engulfed them. If only now he'd give her a future with him. But the day ended and they returned to the farm without an announcement of their engagement.

Wade had left Samson in the barn and Ashby willingly went with him to release the dog. The Newfoundland greeted them happily, then dashed past them as Wade flicked on a light and pulled her inside the door.

"My present to you," he said, as she stared at the object commanding the center of the large room, then turned to him. "It's a headboard," he added, answering what he thought was her silent question.

Ashby forced herself to move forward. The headboard was made from an upside-down tree. The root system spread out like a canopy above the place where the bed would be, then narrowed into a pillar before widening again into branches trimmed to serve as bed posts. "It's beautiful," she said, reaching out to stroke the smooth wood as an excuse to keep her face averted. But her voice lacked conviction as her hopes for a proposal collapsed.

A new thought struck her and she swung around to meet Wade's gaze. "Is it for our marriage bed?"

He crossed the room to join her. His eyes were sad as he reached out and stroked her hair. "Not if you take it to Georgetown."

He spoke softly, but, to Ashby, those few words hit her ears with the force of a sonic boom. She reeled away from him and gripped the pillar of the headboard with both hands. Closing her eyes, she took a deep breath and leaned her forehead against it.

The only sound was that of the wind sneaking through the eaves. A lonely sound, she thought. She'd been so sure that, like her, Wade had spent the last two weeks thinking of ways they could remain together.

"There is such a thing as compromise," she said, shoving aside her disappointment and meeting his waiting gaze.

"A weekend together here and there?" He shook his head. "As happy as I would be to see you, I couldn't bear to see you leave over and over again."

Ashby shook her head. That scenario hadn't even occurred to her. "Why can't we divide the year? Spend part of it here and part of it in Georgetown?"

"Get married?"

She nodded. Wade lifted one hand and massaged the back of his neck, trying to ease muscles stiffening from tension.

"And what would I do in the city?" he asked. "Play househusband? What about the farm? Who would look after that?"

Ashby tightened her grip on the tree trunk, needing its support as she recognized the sarcasm creeping into his voice. "We could spend the winter in Washington. You could hire someone to look after what little has to be done on the farm. And winter is when you make most of your furniture, anyway. I have a basement, you could use that for your workshop."

"You mean sell my furniture?"

She nodded as he stalked away from her and sat down on a stool by his worktable. "I can't make a business out of my furniture, Ashby," he said, his shoulders sagging. "I thought you understood that."

Ashby squeezed her eyes closed, fighting the painful realization that she'd been deceiving herself about their future. She took a deep breath and opened her eyes. "What's wrong with moderation? I'd tie you into an exclusive contract so you couldn't turn it into a big business. And I'd do the promoting, you wouldn't have to get involved in that side of it."

A grin almost made it to Wade's lips as a part of him realized that what he loved most about this woman was the will that matched his own. But his smile died still-born. He'd like an exclusive contract with her, all right—a marriage contract that would keep her on the farm.

"I can't."

"Can't or won't?" she challenged.

He shrugged helplessly. "What's the difference? I have no choice." He rose and advanced toward her.

"So it's over? You're just going to pack me off and wave goodbye?" Ashby backed around the tree trunk, out of his reach.

Wade halted. "If I could, I'd ask you to stay and marry me. But I can't ask you to give up your gallery. It means too much to you. I love you too much to do that to you . . . and I couldn't bear to see your love for me turn to hate." He circled the headboard, but she moved ahead of him.

"If you truly loved me, you'd find a way for us to be together!" She fled toward the door.

"Do you think letting you go is easy for me?" The torture she heard in his voice stopped her, but she didn't turn. She stared in the direction of the door, unable to see it through a misty cloud of tears.

"Going to Washington with you," he said, his voice so low she had to strain to hear him, "would be a death sentence for me. I'm not asking you to give up your gallery to prove your love for me. Do I have to give up my life to prove my love for you?"

His footsteps neared. Ashby pivoted and slammed her open palm against his chest, against the heart he believed prevented them from sharing the rest of their lives. He stood in place as she held him at arm's length. "You don't have to die for me!" she protested, her tears evaporating in the heat of her rising fury. "You can follow your diet and exercise in the city just as easily as you do here."

"No, I can't!" Wade gripped her by the shoulders and shook her until she let her hand fall from his chest. "I've been honest with you, Ashby. Leaving Chicago and my career was not easy for me. I can't go back."

"I'm not asking you to! Washington is not Chicago! Selling your furniture is not the same as trading stocks!"

Wade released her shoulders and dropped his hands to his sides as he shook his head helplessly. "Ashby," he begged, "please, try to understand."

She stared up at him for a moment, the fight draining out of her as she realized that she'd loved and lost. "All I understand," she said bleakly, "is that you're willing to throw away the best thing that's ever happened to me." She paused and from somewhere she found a laugh, a brittle, ironic laugh. "And to you—or so I thought," she added, then turned and stalked out the door.

13

ASHBY WENT TO BED, not caring if Wade joined her or not. She craved the oblivion of sleep, but it would not come. Dry-eyed and awake, she stared into the inky blackness and willed herself not to think of her empty future. Time passed, but she didn't know if it was hours or minutes later when Wade came to her. She rose to meet him and began tugging at his clothes, her movements frenzied with the knowledge that this was her last night with him.

He stilled her hands and, as he slipped out of his clothes, she calmed, understanding that Wade wanted this night to be slow, unhurried. *Yes,* she silently agreed as they returned to the bed and she lit the bedside lamp, *you're right. Each moment, each touch must be savored, for the memory must last a lifetime.*

She stared up at him, imprinting every hard angle of his face and body on her mind. Then she drew him down atop her and they made sweet, silent love. She clung to him afterward, as though his warmth could dispel the cold of the awful emptiness seeping into her soul. Wade held her tightly, periodically squeezing her as if trying to bring her closer yet and she sensed that he, too, wanted to stave off the impending loneliness. Although they slept little, dozing fitfully, they remained silent. There was nothing left to be said.

Wade held her until the first rays of the rising sun lightened the room and he could see her clearly. Lovingly, he stared down at her, memorizing her tousled blond curls, her slightly parted lips still reddened from his kisses, the pert tilt of her small nose, the crescent-shaped fans of her eyelashes. Then he pressed a kiss on her smooth forehead and eased himself away from her.

He'd been a fool to ever become involved with her when he'd known from the start there was no future for their relationship, he told himself as he dressed; but he couldn't bring himself to regret a moment of their summer together. With one last, long look at the small form curled in the middle of his bed, he left the room with Samson at his heels.

Because he loved her, he would let her go. But he needed the solitude of a long walk to find the strength to say goodbye.

Ashby listened to his retreating footsteps. She'd sensed his absence the instant he'd withdrawn his warmth from her side, but rather than call him back she'd let the cold of his abandonment chill her flesh and trickle into her heart. When she was sure he was gone, she rose. Her movements leaden, she showered, dressed . . . and packed.

She didn't leave a note.

SHE DID STOP in Hickory to say goodbye to Millie and Coot. She entered the old house without knocking and found them at the kitchen table. Millie took one look at her face and rose.

"What's wrong?"

Ashby stepped into her embrace without answering. She held on to the older woman with all her strength. Tears welled into a tight, painful knot deep inside her. But she wasn't a little girl who could turn to Mama to solve her problems, and the tears remained unshed. Instead, she took a deep breath and stepped back.

"I'm leaving."

"You're what?" Coot's chair scraped against the linoleum floor as he shoved back from the table and rose to join them. "Dang it, girl! You cain't go nowhere. You belong here with my boy!"

Ashby winced and glanced away from him, unable to meet the accusation in the green eyes so like Wade's.

"Sit down and finish your breakfast," Millie told him. "This is woman talk." Her arm around Ashby, she led her into the living room and sat down beside her on the couch.

"There's not much to say," Ashby said in a dull voice, "except goodbye. Wade won't come with me and—" she lifted her gaze blindly to the ceiling and took a deep breath "—and he won't ask me to stay."

Millie hugged her, then regarded her silently for a moment. "Would you, if he asked?"

"Yes!" The answer tore out of Ashby's throat as an agonized cry, and she jumped to her feet. "He's so high-handed about everything else! He barely gave me any time to think about staying on the farm and he knew I was hesitant about seeing my relatives, but he went ahead and invited them to my birthday party."

She paced in front of the couch, thinking out loud. "But when it comes to planning a future together, he turns noble and refuses to tell me to stay!"

"And what about your gallery?" Millie asked softly. "Could you give it up for him?"

Ashby halted her pacing abruptly, as though she'd run into a wall. She sighed and returned her troubled gaze to the older woman. "I'd like a compromise," she said, sinking back onto the couch. "I have a good manager and don't have to stay in Georgetown all year, but Wade won't consider living in the city, even part-time."

"It was very hard for him to leave it," Millie said, "until he put the decision in terms of life or death. Once he made up his mind, he hasn't looked back. He doesn't think he has a choice."

Ashby jammed her fingers through her hair, then held her head as if it might burst. "I know, I know! He told me about his heart, his damned competitiveness! But I love him and I want to be with him. And he loves me, too!" She dropped her hands, unconsciously holding them out to Millie in a pleading gesture. "Why can't he compromise? He's old enough to have learned from his mistakes. Why do I have to give up everything if we're to stay together?"

Millie took her hands. "Because a woman's place is by her man." She paused as Ashby winced. "At least, it was in my day," she amended. "I was a country girl with no more than a high-school education, but when Abe joined the foreign service I had to learn to relate to people from all over the world."

She paused, her grip on Ashby's hands tightening. "I hated it at first. I was so afraid I'd make a mistake, commit some horrible faux pas that would ruin his career." She smiled, no longer seeing Ashby as she delved into the past. "But Abe had total faith in me and that gave me the strength. I studied books on etiquette and memorized every book on protocol he brought home. I'd ignored proper grammar in high school, but because it was important to Abe it became important to me."

Her eyes were misty when she again focused on Ashby. "I can't tell you what to do, honey. I wish I could. I believe a woman's place is by her man, but you have to do what's right for you. Kay wasn't happy away from the city and I'm sure Wade is afraid you wouldn't be, either. That's why he won't ask you—or tell you—to stay."

Ashby hung her head. Could she be happy without her gallery? She tried to envision a future without it, but it had been too much a part of her for too long. She'd lived without seeing it for almost six weeks, but she'd talked to Joanna frequently. She'd been away from it, but not without it.

"Give Wade, give yourself time," Millie advised. "Go back to your gallery and listen to your heart. Not this." She tapped Ashby's head. "But this." She pressed her hand against her own left breast. "And you'll know what's the right thing to do."

Ashby managed a wan smile. "Thank you," she said, "for everything. You've been so good to me."

As they stood, Coot opened the door that led from the living room to the hallway. "Could barely hear a word," he complained, "jest a mumbling." He turned to his daughter. "Did you talk some sense into the girl's head?"

"Don't mind him," Millie told Ashby, slipping her arm around her waist and leading her to the front door. "He's just a meddlesome old coot."

"She ain't going to stay, then?" He stationed himself at the front door, barring her exit.

"Not this time," Millie said. "Leave her be. She's got to go back to her gallery and let her heart do some talking."

"Kids!" Coot snorted with disgust, but moved away from the door. "Cain't see the way of things and they think they're so durned smart. Should of got old preacher Jenkins down here yestiddy when we had the chance."

Ashby ignored his grumblings and hugged him. "If you decide to sell more crafts in your store, let me know," she said. "I'll still send people your way."

Coot awkwardly patted her on the back. "You jest get yourself back here, girl. I ain't gittin' any younger and I aim to be dancin' at your weddin'."

The tears she'd managed to suppress threatened to spill at his words. Afraid to speak, Ashby nodded and with a final kiss for Millie, she stumbled out the door.

The day was sunny, but she left the top up on her convertible. The brilliant green of the trees covering the mountainsides made no impression on her mind, nor did the bright pinks of the wild roses that sprawled below them. Nor did she put a tape in her tape player. No music could lighten the somber notes of the funeral dirge playing in her head.

She drove slowly, knowing her mind wasn't on her driving. The ache in her chest seemed to grow with each mile she put between herself and Hickory. Wade's green eyes haunted her—twinkling with laughter, heavy-lidded with desire, tender with compassion. She blinked and focused on the road, then saw his large hands, capable and competent as he sanded a tree branch, deft and gentle as he stroked her body.

Traffic was heavy when she hit Washington, forcing her to concentrate. When she pulled to a stop in front of the garage off the alley behind her brick town house, she stared blankly at the closed door. A dog barked and she looked around for Samson, then shook herself. She was home, she realized, and reached into the glove compartment for the garage-door opener.

She pulled the car into the garage, unloaded her suitcases and unlocked the back door to her home. The gallery was closed, the house quiet and dark, as she stepped inside and locked the door behind her. Sunlight peeked around shutters, illuminating the stairs to the upper floor where she lived and she headed straight for them. All she wanted was up there.

Bed. Sleep. Oblivion.

THE SHRIEK of the telephone woke her and she lunged for it with one thought in her mind. Wade. She'd slept poorly, waking when she reached for him and didn't find him, then tossing and turning before exhaustion dragged her back to unconsciousness.

She missed the phone, grabbed for it again and knocked it to the floor. "Hello! I'm here, hang on!" she yelled, rolling onto the floor after the phone.

"Ashby? Are you all right?" Joanna's voice, laden with concern, greeted her as she at last got the receiver to her ear.

"Yes. What time is it?" She'd left the shutters closed and the room was dark.

"Almost noon. I saw your car in the garage and got worried when you didn't come down. I knocked, but the door was locked and you didn't answer."

"I got in late last night," she lied, rather than explain how little sleep she'd gotten the night before. Wade, what was he doing now? Eating lunch in his kitchen with Samson at his feet? Did he miss her?

"Sorry I woke you, then," Joanna was saying. "Go back to sleep."

"No, I'll be down as soon as I clean up." She had to keep busy, Ashby told herself, as she hung up and headed toward the shower. She couldn't think about

Wade. Couldn't linger in bed and feel sorry for herself. She had an exhibit to organize and advertise. A lot of good people had put their faith and trust in her and she couldn't let them down, no matter how much of a shambles she'd made of her personal life.

Her stomach rumbled as she made her way down the stairs, reminding her that she hadn't eaten the previous day. The thought of food was unappealing and she stopped in the kitchen to feed it the coffee she knew Joanna would have made. Her gaze took in the sight of the galley-size kitchen she'd designed herself when she'd ripped out the original to make more room for the gallery.

Although small, it was efficiently organized with more than adequate counter space on each side of the center aisle and she knew from experience that it was as capable of producing hundreds of hors d'oeuvres for an opening as an intimate dinner for two.

She'd always thought it sleek and modern looking. But today, the almond countertops and matching Formica cabinets looked cold and institutional, with none of the warmth of the oak in Wade's kitchen.

Shoving herself away from the counter, Ashby carried her coffee mug into the gallery. Joanna flashed her a quick smile as she handed a customer a brochure on one of the current artists on exhibit.

Sipping at her coffee, Ashby wandered through the open room, reacquainting herself with the displays. She'd chosen a Southwestern theme for this exhibit. Framed paintings featured desert and canyon scenes. Sculptures depicted buffalo, horses, Indians, stagecoaches and cowboys. Native American pottery and kachina dolls perched on tables and shelves.

A flower-shop owner she knew had loaned her cactus plants to add to the atmosphere and she smiled when she saw that one bore a Sold tag, pleased that she'd made a sale for a friend. But her smile was short-lived as her gaze fell on a handwoven wall hanging and she remembered the Navajo rugs on Wade's hardwood floors.

If there was no relief from thoughts of Wade in her gallery, where would she find it? She turned at the sound of the chimes she'd hung at the entrance and saw that Joanna's customer had left.

"You've done well without me," she said to the tall redhead. "Most of these are not the pieces we had up when I left."

Joanna smiled proudly. "Want to take a look at the books?"

Ashby shook her head. "Not today. My head feels foggy."

Joanna eyed her curiously. "You *must* be in love," she decided. "Where are you hiding this hunk with the delicious voice? You don't think I called so often just to talk to you, do you?" She didn't notice her boss wince and hide her face behind her coffee cup. "When do I get to meet him?"

"He doesn't like the city much." Ashby tried for a nonchalant shrug as she set her mug on the glass counter. "How are the jewelry sales going?" She pretended interest in the display on the velvet-lined shelves underneath the counter. Freshwater pearls, coral and turquoise mingled with feathered earrings and liquid silver necklaces.

"Uh-oh. I smell trouble in the romance department." Ashby looked up to see sympathy in her friend's brown eyes. "Let's close for lunch and you can tell Aunt Joanna all about it."

"No, you go ahead." If Wade's mother hadn't been able to help her, how could Joanna? "I'll mind the store." Joanna hesitated, but Ashby moved behind the counter, found her purse and handed it to her. "Go. I owe you a lot more than a long lunch break for the time I've been away. But that will be a start."

Joanna took her purse reluctantly. "Promise to remember I have a soft shoulder when you need it?" Ashby nodded.

Her friend respected her silence on the subject of Wade when she returned from lunch, but her sister Sue showed no such consideration when she burst through the door.

"How could you have left that man without so much as a note?" she demanded in lieu of a greeting, heedless of the attentive ears of not only Joanna but several customers. "Not to mention the three brothers and two sisters expecting to meet you for breakfast! When you didn't show up at the motel, I called Wade and the poor man had to tell me you'd left!"

Ashby gaped at her sister, dismayed that she'd forgotten about the breakfast date with her family. She'd call and apologize, but her first priority was to get Sue in private where she could hear more about Wade.

"What did Wade say?" Ashby asked, as she led her sister to the kitchen.

"Not much. He came back from a walk and you were gone. He called his mother and she told him you'd left for Georgetown. He was very sorry about breakfast. He'd forgotten about it, too, and was sure you'd be in touch with us. He sounded awful.

"And you don't look any better." Sue pressed her face up close to Ashby's to get a better look. "That white stuff under your eyes doesn't hide those shadows."

"Thanks," Ashby said, pouring two cups of coffee and handing her one. She crossed to the small bay off the kitchen that served as her dining room and sat down at the table. She stared at the one tree in her small backyard and thought of the view from Wade's front porch.

Sue followed her and sat down opposite her, obstructing her view of the tree. Ashby shifted so she could see around her.

"Quit staring out the window like a zombie, Ashby. You're scaring me."

Ashby ducked her head guiltily and sipped her coffee. "I'm sorry. Did Wade say anything else?"

"You didn't take your birthday present, but I was to tell you he'd send it."

Ashby jerked with surprise and spilled her coffee. "I don't want it! How could he do that to me?"

Sue tossed some napkins over the spill as she rounded the table to slide her arm around Ashby's shoulders. "What happened?"

Ashby yanked herself out of Sue's grasp, stood and faced her sister. "He made me a headboard for my birthday!" she shouted, the emotions churning within her coalescing into anger and frustration. "For a bed he'll never share! I wanted a marriage proposal and I got an empty bed!"

Sue took a step backward. "I'm sorry," Ashby said in a lower voice. "I shouldn't take it out on you." She sank back into her chair, her anger evaporating as quickly as it had risen.

"Start at the beginning and tell me about it," Sue said and sat down, too.

Ashby did, but Sue had no more of an answer for her than Millie. Even less, for Sue knew better how much her gallery meant to her. "Give him time," she finally advised. "He loves you. A blind man could have seen it every time he looked at you at the party. And he's hurting now. I could hear it in his voice. He'll change his mind and compromise, you'll see."

Ashby accepted Sue's hug, but couldn't share her optimism. How could she compete with Wade's dedication to his life-style? How could she give up her gallery? How could she live without Wade? The questions lurked in her heart as she dragged through her days.

When a huge carton from Wade arrived at the gallery, Ashby told Joanna to store it in the basement with her other pieces from West Virginia. No note accompanied it and she couldn't bear to look at the headboard. She would, she'd decided, exhibit it, then store it again.

Joanna wanted her to check their inventory to be sure that everything shipped was what she'd ordered, but Ashby had yet to set foot in the basement. Every piece would remind her of Wade, of looking up into his green eyes as she shopped, of feeling his large hand spanning her waist as they walked, of seeing the wind ruffle his dark hair as he drove her car.

"There's a quilt rack with it," Joanna said, when she returned from the basement, "and this."

Ashby turned from the cash register to see her manager holding the blue teddy bear that Wade had won for her at the Independence Day fair. She stared at it as Joanna set it on the counter and saw Wade on the merry-go-round, heard his whoop as his mount lifted his feet off the floor.

"A little cross-eyed, but cute," Joanna commented.

Ashby reached for the bear and held it against her breasts. She'd named it Wade, Jr., and she'd intentionally left it behind, not wanting the reminder that the toy was the only Junior she'd ever give Wade. Abruptly, she thrust it away from her and dropped it in the trash. Joanna gave a strangled cry, but Ashby turned her back on her, refusing to give her an explanation.

Later, as she prepared for bed, the memory of the blue bear in the wicker trash basket pulled her back down the stairs like a magnet. Try as she might, she couldn't banish Wade from her mind. Why, then, she reasoned, should she deny herself the pleasure of holding the fuzzy toy? With the bear tucked against her breasts, Ashby slept better that night than she had in the two weeks since she'd left Hickory.

As THE HIGH HUMIDITY and temperatures of a Washington summer dropped with the advance of September, Ashby confided in Joanna. She felt she owed her an explanation for failing to resume her former responsibilities and for extending the Southwestern show to delay the folk-art exhibit until November. Only the memory of the hope and pride in humble eyes like Anna's prevented her from canceling it altogether.

Content to let her manager run the business, Ashby barely summoned enough energy to talk to customers and ring up sales. Joanna planned the promotion for the upcoming folk-art exhibit and drafted a letter to the craftspeople for Ashby's signature that explained the postponement as a decision made to link it to the Thanksgiving and Christmas season. She also contracted with a more avant-garde artist for the next exhibit to begin in January. She asked for advice, but Ashby granted her approval as automatically as a rubber stamp . . . and gave her a raise.

A shy call from Anna, Wade's cousin, roused her from her lethargy. "John has some vacation time coming," Anna explained, "and we was thinking maybe we'd come see my quilts hanging in your gallery, if that would be all right."

Ashby assured her it was, glancing guiltily at the invitations to the opening Joanna had put on her desk that she'd yet to address. "The customers like to meet the artists."

"Don't know as I'm an artist," Anna said, "and don't know what I'd say to rich city folk. I jes' want to see my quilts a-hangin' in your gallery."

"You *are* an artist and you'd say the same things you say to me," Ashby said, and then she asked after Wade.

"Don't see him much. No one does. He seems to be sticking pretty close to home. Thought you two was good together, not that it's any of my business."

"We were, Anna, we were." Ashby tugged at her hair, half expecting to feel the curls Wade liked, but she'd had it cut and resumed the daily straightening process. "If you see him, would you tell him I miss him?"

"Well, sure." Anna faltered, apparently surprised at the request. "Cain't you tell him yourself?"

"I—I haven't heard from him."

Anna laughed. "Well, girl, you got his number, don't you? Why're you talking to me when it's him you want?"

Weakly, Ashby agreed and they said goodbye. Anna was right, she thought; she could call Wade. The longing to hear his voice made her lift the receiver. What could she say that she hadn't already said? She was willing to compromise; he was the one who had to relent if they were to be together again. Her hand dropped back down onto her desk.

No, she couldn't call him...but she could invite him to the exhibit opening. And Coot and Millie, too.

Thoughts of seeing Wade again filled her with excitement. She attacked the stack of invitations, addressing Wade's first, then ground to an abrupt halt, still not knowing what to say. She pulled out a blank sheet of paper and drafted note after note, but each one sounded either too casual or too desperate. Finally, she added just one word to the invitation.

Please.

14

A GLORIOUS INDIAN summer graced Washington in October, but Ashby barely noticed. Wade hadn't responded to her invitation. She pictured him walking with Samson, pondering what to do as he gazed at the panoramic views tinged now with the reds and golds of autumn. Although tempted, she refused to call him. The next move was his. It would be like him to decide to surprise her by showing up, she assured herself repeatedly, but the refrain faded into a murmur as November neared.

She struggled through her days, spending her mornings in anticipation of the arrival of the mail and the afternoons in disappointment. Nights, she spent with the blue teddy bear, whose fur was wearing as thin as her hopes. Sundays, she sat by her telephone, steadfastly refusing Joanna's and Sue's invitations to socialize. Coot and Millie called to say they'd come to the opening, but could tell her little about Wade. Like Anna, they rarely saw him.

By November, Ashby felt as bereft as the trees stripped of their leaves. She clung to the hope that Wade would surprise her by showing up at the exhibit opening, scheduled for the week before Thanksgiving, but never in her wildest dreams did she expect a shipment of his furniture to arrive.

No wonder his relatives hadn't seen much of him, she thought in amazement, as she unpacked a settee, a

dining-room set and a slate-topped desk with a coor-
dinating chair. He'd been spending all his time in his
workshop. She stroked the smooth wood enviously,
knowing it had recently experienced his touch.

But what did his sending of the furniture mean? Obviously he'd changed his mind about selling, but she
looked in vain for a note. Which meant, she decided,
the furniture itself was her answer. He was coming to
the opening!

In a fever of excitement, she revised her exhibit arrangement to make room for Wade's furniture. A bed
with his headboard made up with one of Anna's quilts
sat in the middle of the large open room. Handmade
teddy bears lounged across the pillow shams. His quilt
rack leaned against a nearby wall.

A kerosene lantern with a ceramic, hand-thrown
base sat atop a tatted doily on the slate-topped desk.
Carved wooden candlesticks decked his dining-room
table. The apple dolls and quilted pillows stood in a row
along the back of the settee. Wreaths, framed embroi-
dery, woven rugs and more quilts hung on the walls.
Hooked rugs warmed the floor. Corn-husk dolls stood
on the mantel above a fireplace.

She chose an autumnal decor for opening night. The
scent of hot apple cider permeated the air and handwoven baskets filled with pumpkins, colorful gourds
and the scarlet-orange of dried sugar maple leaves dotted the room. The menu was simple country fare, much
like the picnics she'd attended with Wade. And her invitations had emphasized informal attire rather than
black tie.

The room was more cluttered than usual, Ashby saw,
as she nervously fluffed the curls framing her face and
waited for the first arrivals to the exhibit opening, but

it was a browser's delight—warm and homey in contrast to the early dark of a cloudy, misty November evening. She would be proud to share it with Wade.

WADE HIT THE CAPITAL Beltway circling the city late enough, he'd thought, to miss the rush-hour traffic. He was wrong. Cars still clogged the multilane highway, traveling bumper to bumper at dangerous speeds. Despite his years of experience driving Chicago's expressways, he felt his hands on the steering wheel grow clammy and his heart pound, his senses overwhelmed by the sheer number of cars. But a quick glance at his watch told him he had no time to waste if he wanted to see Ashby before the opening. The last thing he wanted was an audience of strangers inhibiting her response to him.

His old instincts kicked into gear as he floored the accelerator of the big truck and forced his way into the steady stream of traffic. Once in place, he eased his pressure on the accelerator only slightly. He'd made the agonizing decision to attend the opening less than an hour before he'd left and now he was in a fever of impatience to see Ashby, a fever fed by the frantic pulse of city traffic. Adrenaline pumped through his veins as he maneuvered the truck to the express lanes at the extreme left of the highway.

He drove aggressively, as he always had in the city, and he found the size of his vehicle a welcome advantage over the sleek sports cars he used to favor. Drivers of compacts, he noticed, seemed to move over more quickly when they saw the Ford truck looming in their rearview mirrors. When they didn't move fast enough, he cursed, blew his horn and switched his headlights on and off to make sure they were aware of his presence on their bumper.

When one driver rolled down his window and shook his fist at him, then braked in warning rather than switching lanes, Wade had to force himself to slow his speed rather than hit him. And the depth of his desire to ram that car frightened him.

With conscious effort, he eased his pressure on the accelerator and began moving back to the slower, right-hand lane. Dear God, he swore, what was happening to him? Ten minutes back into the city and he'd resumed his old, aggressive, competitive habits.

Keep calm, he ordered himself. *Take it easy. This is what you left behind. Haven't you learned anything in four years of living in peace and quiet on the farm?*

But when he was off the beltway and in the city on Wisconsin Avenue, his senses were further assaulted. Drivers raced traffic signals or pulled out of side streets directly in front of him, sirens echoed, horns blared, pedestrians jaywalked, kids dashed out at red lights to wash his windshield and demand money, buses belched exhaust and stopped at every block, slowing his progress in the right-hand lane he'd forced himself to take.

Patience, he urged himself. *Ashby will be at the gallery all night.* But his courtesy toward merging cars forced him into the inner lane at a circular intersection and trapped him in a seemingly endless circuit of the rotary. Claustrophobia threatened as he missed his exit, time and time again.

When he finally escaped, he was sweating—and cursing the city, other drivers and Ashby. And he quickly discovered that he'd taken the wrong exit off the circle and in his attempt to find his way back to

Wisconsin Avenue, he went the wrong way down a one-way street.

Swearing still more, he pulled into an alley by a house to turn around. A man opened the front door to an adjacent house and Wade rolled down his window, eager to ask directions to Georgetown.

"Hey, stupid, get outta my driveway!" the man yelled before Wade could speak. "Can't you dumb tourists read road signs? This is a one-way street."

Half-maddened by frustration, Wade swung out of his truck, his hands balled into fists, the man's rude hostility snapping his frayed temper.

"Get outta here before I call the cops!" the man added hastily, backing through his door and slamming it.

Wade glared in impotent fury at the man's closed door, then took a deep breath and slowly climbed back into his truck. The late-afternoon clouds had darkened with the arrival of early evening and mist moistened his windshield. Switching on lights and wipers, he backed out of the man's driveway and worked his way back to Wisconsin Avenue.

As soon as he hit M Street and found a spot, he parked, then sat for long moments, his hands still gripping the steering wheel as he leaned his forehead against it. The city, he mused, brought out the worst in some people. Aggression in him, paranoia in others. Sighing, he got out of the truck and slipped into his parka. As he closed and locked the door, he stared at the suit jacket and tie lying on the front seat. With a shake of his head, he turned and strode down the street.

WHEN COOT AND MILLIE arrived with Anna and her husband, John, Ashby met them at the door and looked past them, expecting to see Wade's big frame. She didn't. Nor was there any sign of him on the busy cobblestone street.

"We'll talk later," Millie said and hugged her as Ashby's welcoming smile faltered.

"Wade didn't come?" Ashby asked, still looking beyond them. Of course, he was coming, she answered herself. He'd sent her his furniture. He was parking the car on a side street; that was why she didn't see him.

"Danged boy won't leave his farm," Coot said, tugging at the collar of his shirt as if strangled by the tie at his throat. "Don't never come to Sunday dinner, neither. Moping like a baby." He peered at Ashby. "You're looking a bit peaked, too."

"Thank you," Ashby said. So certain that Wade would be with them, she was slow to absorb what Coot had said. She stared blindly at the old man.

Joanna shut the door as she joined them and introduced herself to the new arrivals. "Let me take your coats. Would you like something to eat or drink?" Ashby remained in place, staring at the door as Joanna led her friends away.

Wade wasn't coming. He wouldn't be drinking the applejack she'd scoured the city to find. The realization seemed to open a hole in her heart and she turned, very slowly and very carefully, away from the door. Feeling as fragile as a teacup threaded with hairline cracks, she followed her friends from Hickory to the buffet table.

RAIN DRIPPED OFF the tree above him and onto his unprotected head, but Wade barely noticed as he stared across the cobblestone street and watched the door of the red-brick town house bearing the sign, The Ashby White Gallery, close behind his family. He'd edged farther behind the tree trunk when he saw Ashby peer out the open door and down the street.

When she disappeared inside he stepped forward again and gazed at the two-story building. Carefully hidden spotlights illuminated the black door and the sign above it. Colorful Indian corn hung below the brass knocker. He need only cross the street and lift that knocker and the woman he loved would open the door.

But he didn't. Instead, he looked through the big bay window and saw Ashby move through the brightly lit room, her hair curling softly around her delicate face, her figure small and curvy beneath the elegance of the sophisticated blue suit she wore. She smiled up at men and women alike—cool, calm and collected, unaffected by his absence.

What would she do if he walked in? he wondered. Give him that same polished smile? Say, "How nice to see you, again?" Or would she tell him she still loved him?

He didn't know—would never know. He couldn't share her world, not even part-time. He'd thought he could when he sent her his furniture; thought he could spend the winters in the city and busy himself with his craft. But he didn't dare.

His aggressive driving was but a portent of the personality traits that would recur if he returned to the city. Its ceaseless activity created a hum of excitement in the air that tugged at forces within him that had lain dormant for four years. But he felt them as strongly as he ever had.

The drive to succeed, to *excel*, burned within him. As much as he loved Ashby, her small gallery could never contain him. He'd fuel her idle dreams of expanding and throw himself into negotiations, wheeling and dealing himself into an early death. A city was a place of power and he couldn't live there without securing a piece of it for himself.

The farm was different. It kept him humble, for even he accepted that he had no power over the elements. And he had no choice but to return there. Alone.

He turned away from the tree and made his way back to his truck, unaware that the moisture on his cheeks was warmer than the rain.

ASHBY GOT THROUGH the evening, but she wasn't sure how. She felt as if a robot had taken her place, making all the appropriate, polite responses when addressed, while the real Ashby White watched from afar.

She'd returned Millie and Coot's hospitality by inviting them to stay at her town house, but hadn't had room to include Anna and John. Thankful that she only had to face two sets of sympathetic eyes, she pleaded tiredness when they were alone. She led them to their rooms, then fled to the refuge of her own. She couldn't bear looking into the green eyes so like Wade's.

"Why would Wade change his mind about selling his furniture, then not come to see me?" she burst out the next morning when Millie and Coot joined her for breakfast. She'd alternated between anger and tears throughout the night, yet hadn't come up with an answer.

"He's a proud man," Millie said, setting down her coffee cup. "I told you, once he made up his mind to leave the city, he hasn't looked back."

"But he changed his mind about the furniture!"

Millie nodded. "Maybe the next move is yours."

"You mean call him?"

"Only you can decide that."

"Been thinking 'bout your idea for my store." Coot joined the conversation as he finished his omelet and pushed away his empty plate. Irritated at his change of subject, Ashby listened with half an ear, her mind still fixed on Wade. "Millie's done picked out some of the local craft work and what tourists that do stop in been buying 'em right quick."

He tugged at the opening of his cardigan sweater as though looking for the straps of his bib overalls. "Seems like the best I could do for the local folk is find me someone with your know-how to get the word out and bring in more of the city folk. Think you know anyone who might be interested in buying the store?"

"You want to give it up?" Ashby asked, surprised out of her private thoughts. Coot thrived on the daily contact with his customers.

"Wouldn't mind still working there," he admitted. "Mebbe you could find me more like a partner. I'd do the sellin' and the other could do the advertisin'. Probably ain't too many city folk want to move to Hickory, nohow."

Ashby studied his lined face and guileless green eyes. "I might," she said slowly, suspecting that he hadn't really changed the subject, "just know somebody. I'll have to get back to you, okay?"

"Sure enough." Coot cackled cheerfully and the familiar sound brought a smile to Ashby's lips, but her expression was pensive as she cleaned up the kitchen after they left. They'd planned to stay another day, but a forecast of snow in the mountains changed their plans. She'd objected halfheartedly, yet hadn't insisted, knowing she was too preoccupied with thoughts of Wade to be a good hostess.

There was nothing preoccupied or pensive about her actions in the following weeks. She didn't, however, call Wade. He'd let her stew in her own juice long enough and she decided to give him a dose of his own medicine. The delivery of his furniture had thrown the ball into her court and she'd give him no say in the decisions she was making.

"I suggest you change the gallery to a Christmas decor in the first week of December," she told Joanna, after she'd taken her into her confidence and her friend had readily agreed to a new business arrangement, "and finalize the contract for the new exhibit in January."

Ashby had no desire to deal with the artist, who billed himself as Pierre, although his name was Sam. Like his paintings and unlike the craftspeople from West Virginia, he was bold and brassy. He'd made passes at both Joanna and her and acted as though he were doing them a favor by allowing them to exhibit his work.

Winter in Washington seemed to conspire with her rather than against her. Dreary November days drifted into dreary December days. A light snowstorm brightened the city streets for a few hours, but traffic quickly turned it a dirty gray.

She wrote her Christmas cards early, eager to cement her new ties to her extended family in Weathersfield, and her optimism was rewarded by their responses. She didn't send to Wade and he didn't send to her.

She sold her Porsche and bought a four-wheel-drive truck like Wade's, only red. Pretty as well as practical, and perfect for Christmas. With that, she was ready.

THE TRUCK WAS FUN to drive and held to the snow-slickened roads very well, although Ashby was careful to keep the salesman's admonition in mind—nothing, not even four-wheel drive, helped on ice. She reached her destination as planned, on the twilight of Christmas Eve, and parked in the garage.

Her co-conspirators were waiting for her and went out of their way to soothe her nerves. Ashby accepted their fussing and the hot chocolate they offered, but felt totally calm. She knew what she was doing was right for her and felt prepared to live with the consequences.

At the sound of the front door opening, she took the place assigned to her and listened to the tread of familiar footsteps approaching. Her calm ebbed, washed away by a tide of excitement, and she clasped her hands in front of her to hide their trembling. She was sure the thumping of her heart against her ribs outperformed the beat of the Christmas carol, "The Little Drummer Boy," playing on the stereo.

"Merry—" Wade's greeting faltered as he stepped into Millie and Coot's darkened living room and saw Ashby. She stood in the glow of the illuminated Christmas tree, her blond hair shining like a halo about her head. He blinked, sure he was hallucinating. "Christmas," he finished saying, still staring, but she didn't disappear. Dancing flames of light flickered from the fireplace, the only movement in the room as he stood still.

"Goldurn it, boy!" Coot's voice emanated from the shadowed couch. "You gonna stand there all night? That's mistletoe hanging above her head. Do I have to turn on the lights for you to do something about it?"

Wade stepped forward, his arms reaching toward Ashby. The gaily-wrapped packages he held slid to the floor and he stumbled over one, but kept moving.

Ashby needed no more invitation than those open arms, and she met him halfway. Rather than bend, he lifted her as he covered her mouth with his and crushed her against his wide chest. He gentled his embrace as he savored her kiss, drinking in the flavor of hot chocolate, the familiar scent of her light perfume, the feel of her fragile curves against him.

Ashby clung to him fiercely, welcoming the strength of his arms around her, the scrape of his hair-roughened chin against her skin, the crisp, clean smell of the outdoors that hung on his clothes. Her lips parted beneath his, but he raised his head.

"Do I get to unwrap this present, later?" he asked in a whisper, afraid to assume too much after her long, silent absence. She nodded and his large hands stroked her back meaningfully as he set her down. *You'll be my favorite present,* he told her silently, *even though I'll have to return you after the holidays.* He'd face the pain of losing her again—later.

Ashby smiled up at him, her heart too full for words. He was even bigger and more handsome than she remembered. Yes, she loved him, stubborn mule that he was. And he still loved her, she was sure of it. Maybe, just maybe, this Christmas she could have her cake and eat it, too.

"Well, that's enough of the huggin' and kissin'," Coot announced, limping over to the Christmas tree. "You can set down and moon over one another whilst we open the presents."

"I hope mine isn't breakable," Millie added dryly. "The one Wade stepped on has my name on it." She knelt by the tree and laid his packages beneath it.

Wade chose a chair by the fireplace and sat down, pulling Ashby into his lap. "Hand them out, Coot," he said, "but I've got all I want, right here."

Coot poked under the tree, muttering to himself. "Where'd you hide it, girl?" he said to Millie, who looked at him without comprehension. He shoved packages aside without any consideration for their wrappings or contents, then pulled out a green envelope with a red bow on it. He handed it to Ashby with a flourish. "We always start with the youngest," he explained.

Ashby took it with trembling fingers, guessing what it might be. Wade watched with interest, realizing that her visit was a surprise only to him. Coot stood over them, jiggling from one foot to the other, as impatient as a schoolboy, while Ashby fumbled with the envelope. Millie moved to stand beside Coot.

Ashby opened the flap and pulled out a single sheet of paper. The title to the store. Her vision blurred as she looked up at Coot. "But..." Her voice failed her. She'd intended on buying a half interest in the store, Coot knew that.

"What the hell?" Wade snatched the paper from her fingers as he read it over her shoulder. "You're giving her the store?"

Ashby rose and hugged Coot, then turned to Wade. He stared at her, his expression so thunderstruck she felt a quiver of doubt. She believed the shipment of his furniture had been his way of telling her he wanted a future with her. Had she been wrong?

"I'm turning the store into a country craft center," she explained nervously. "But I meant to buy a half interest in it." Unable to bear Wade's blank stare, she turned to Coot and held out the title. "I can't accept this. We made a deal."

"Too late now. You got it." Coot stuck his hands behind his back, refusing to take the sheet of paper. "Besides, if'n this dumbbell of a grandson comes to his senses, it'll be yours, anyways."

"Wait a minute, now," Wade said, leaning forward in his chair. He shifted his gaze from Ashby to a smirking Coot and then to his smiling mother. "What exactly is going on here?" His normally quick mind, he decided, had turned to mush the moment he'd seen Ashby, and he wasn't about to make any assumptions before he had all the information he needed.

Tongue-tied by her mounting panic, Ashby couldn't answer. Wasn't it obvious? she wailed inwardly. *I love you, I'm here to stay and I want to marry you!*

"Ashby is moving to Hickory," Millie enunciated the words very carefully, as if speaking to a simpleton, "and she's taking over Coot's store."

Wade looked to Ashby for confirmation. She nodded and quailed inwardly as he leaned back in his chair, apparently giving this news careful consideration.

"What about your gallery?" he asked, his eyes narrowing.

"I offered Joanna a working partnership. I'll have a say in major decisions, but she'll take care of the daily operation." Her hands knotted into fists at her sides as she struggled to still her trembling. She'd considered the possibility that Wade would no longer want her, she reminded herself. And decided that she still wanted to live in Hickory and run the store.

But she'd been so sure that he loved her.

Wade's gaze bored into hers. "I can't let you give up your gallery for me."

Ashby hesitated, her gaze swerving to Coot and Millie. Millie took her father's arm and dragged him from the room.

"I'm not asking for your permission." Ashby dug deeply within herself and found her pride. "And I'm not giving up the gallery. I'm sharing it."

Wade longed to haul her into his arms, but he couldn't. Not yet. There was something he had to hear her say first.

"The folk art has meant more to me than any exhibit I've ever done," she continued, her chin lifting with the defiant tilt he remembered so well from their first meeting. "But I don't expect you to understand that. You couldn't be bothered to come and see it!"

"You didn't call me when you received my furniture!" Wade's temper rose to meet hers. He swung out of his chair and loomed over her. "I missed you and wanted to work out a future with you and all I got was a signed shipping invoice!"

"You didn't enclose a note!" Ashby resisted the urge to back up a step. "How was I supposed to know what was going on in that thick head of yours? I thought the furniture was your way of saying you were coming to the opening!"

"I did! I stood out in the rain and watched you through the window!"

Ashby opened, then closed her mouth, aborting the hot tirade she'd been about to launch. "Why...?" She shook her head in confusion. "Why didn't you come in?"

"Because the second I hit that city, I turned into a maniac!" Wade drew a ragged breath and lowered his voice. "I thought I could stay with you in the winter and only sell my furniture through your gallery. But I realized that if I came in, I'd never go back to the farm. I could *taste* the need in me. I was ready to take over your gallery and turn it into the biggest in the country."

He shook his head, his gaze sliding away from her, into a place she knew she couldn't follow. "And I knew I'd wind up in a hospital again," he continued, returning his focus to her face. "The doctors warned me. The next time I wouldn't walk out—I'd be carried out in a box."

"I'm not asking you to move to Georgetown with me," Ashby assured him softly. "Or to expand my gallery. All I want to do is turn Coot's Country Store into a center for folk art." *And to marry you*, she added silently.

Wade longed to swing her over his shoulder and carry her off to his farm, caveman-style, but she hadn't said the right words. "I can't let you give up your gallery for me," he repeated instead. The memory of Kay's unhappiness was still fresh. He couldn't, wouldn't do that to Ashby. He couldn't bear to see the love in her eyes when she looked at him turn to hate—and worse, indifference.

"I'm not doing it for you!" she insisted. "I'm doing it for people like Anna and for *myself*. If you don't want me—" her voice almost broke, but she steadied it quickly "—just say so. I can live above the store."

"The hell you will!" Wade more than raised his voice, he roared as he heard the words he'd longed to hear. "If you're coming back to West Virginia because that's where you want to be, you'll stay with me!"

Ashby's jaw dropped open, then she snapped it shut as the full import of his words hit her. "Am I to assume that was," she asked primly, "in your usual arrogant fashion, a marriage proposal?"

Laughing as loudly as he'd yelled, Wade swept her up into his arms and twirled her in circles before setting her down. "Damn right, lovely one," he said. "All I had to know was you want to be here as much for yourself as for me." He lowered his lips down to hers.

"So when's the weddin'?" Coot asked as he burst into the room followed by a beaming Millie. "I ain't gettin' any younger!"

Wade raised his head and looked questioningly down at Ashby. "You mean I get a say in this?" she asked with exaggerated surprise.

Wade grinned. "As long as it's preceded by yes."

"You mean she ain't said yes, yet?"

Rather than turn to Coot, Ashby kept her gaze fixed on Wade and pretended to ponder her decision.

"I'll let you sell my furniture in Coot's store," Wade added, his smug grin telling her he knew she needed no extra persuasion.

"In *that* case," Ashby said emphatically, as if his offer had made up her mind, "I'll marry you." She smiled back at Wade before turning to Coot. "And your answer as to when is as soon as my brothers and sisters can get here!"

HER SISTER WILMA had already returned from her sabbatical in France and her brother Bill made it to West Virginia from Alaska in a scant two weeks. Poinsettias still adorned the little white clapboard church in Weathersfield, where Ashby's parents had been married and their children baptized, when Ashby walked down the aisle to meet Wade. Choosing to carry on tradition, she wore the ivory satin dress worn by her grandmother and mother.

The church was filled with family, Ashby saw proudly, as her gaze wandered over the smiling faces turned toward her, then settled on Wade. Breathtakingly handsome in a black tuxedo, he waited for her at the front of the church with their attendants, her brothers and sisters.

She hadn't wanted to choose among her brothers to give her away, but she didn't walk alone. Coot escorted her. "Now, get my Millie some grandkids," he whispered as she kissed his cheek before he handed her over to Wade.

Wade heard him and grinned. "We'll get cracking on it," he promised, as he slipped his arm around Ashby. His gaze held hers, full of promise. "Tonight."

Ashby smiled up at him, her heart filled with love and happiness. There was no almost, she thought, in the heaven of husband, family and career she'd found in Wild, Wonderful West Virginia.

For Temptation, 1993 is the Year of Rebels & Rogues.

Look for twelve stirring stories, one each month, featuring tough-minded, but tenderhearted men. The tempting fulfilment of every woman's fantasy.

With authors like:

Jayne Ann Krentz
Barbara Delinsky
JoAnn Ross

. . . you will meet men like:

Josh – who swore never to play the hero
Cameron – a rogue not of this world
Nick – a rebel with a cause

Twelve Rebels and Rogues – men who are rough around the edges, but incredibly sexy. Men of charm, yet ready to fight for the love of a very special woman . . .

Don't let any of these terrific men get away!

Starting in January 1993   Price: £1.75

Available from Boots, Martins, John Menzies, W.H. Smith, most supermarkets and other paperback stockists.

Also available from Mills & Boon Reader Service, PO Box 236, Thornton Road, Croydon, Surrey CR9 3RU.
(UK Postage & Packing free)

This month's irresistible novels from

—TEMPTATION—

TAKING A CHANCE ON LOVE by Gina Wilkins
The first in her *Veils & Vows* wedding trilogy

Chance Cassidy was hell-bent on saving his impulsive younger brother, Phillip, from making the biggest mistake of his life—marriage. But then he met the bride's aunt, Liz Archer. If he stopped the wedding, would he also stop any chance he had with Liz?

CHRISTMAS KNIGHT by Carin Rafferty

Adam Worth was way behind schedule and he just had to find a Santa Claus and children's photographer—fast. Then Christy Knight walked into his office, the sexiest photographer Santa ever had, and charmed Adam into hiring her and her father. But just what had Adam got himself into?

FIRST AND FOREVER by Katherine Kendall

Laura Daniels had everything she ever dreamed of—everything except a man. Then one moonlit evening, Laura glanced out of her window and there he was. The man to fire her fantasies lived in the apartment across the street. She *had* to meet him . . . .

HEART TROUBLE by Sharon Mayne

Ashby White's sophisticated sex appeal was more than Wade Masters could resist. But city and country life couldn't mix and he knew that no matter how passionate their affair, he couldn't consider any future between them. But could he imagine one apart?

Spoil yourself next month
with these four novels from

— TEMPTATION —

THE PRIVATE EYE by Jayne Ann Krentz

Meet Josh January—the first in Temptation's sinfully sexy
line-up of men under the banner *Rebels & Rogues*. He was a
burned-out rogue of a private eye whose last case nearly killed
him. What had he to offer Maggie Gladstone who so badly
wanted to believe in heroes?

WILD THING by Lynn Patrick

Seth Heller must have been out of his mind to hire drifter
Jassy Reed. He didn't trust anyone—especially women—but
this devil-may-care female aroused his protective—and
predatory—instincts.

ANYTHING GOES by Vickie Lewis Thompson

Strange men started following Laura Rhodes the minute she
arrived in San Francisco. Then, the man she planned to marry
cleared out of town. She was stranded, until devastating Nick
Hooper rode gallantly to her rescue!

ANOTHER RAINBOW by Lynda Trent

When Rainie Sheenan stumbled upon a handsome loner in the
mountains above her home, she couldn't believe her good
fortune. Eligible men were hard to come by, but could she get
past his stubborn resistance?

For Temptation, 1993 is the Year of Rebels & Rogues.

Look for twelve stirring stories, one each month, featuring tough-minded, but tenderhearted men. The tempting fulfilment of every woman's fantasy.

With authors like:

Jayne Ann Krentz
Barbara Delinsky
JoAnn Ross

. . . you will meet men like:

Josh – who swore never to play the hero
Cameron – a rogue not of this world
Nick – a rebel with a cause

Twelve Rebels and Rogues – men who are rough around the edges, but incredibly sexy. Men of charm, yet ready to fight for the love of a very special woman . . .

Don't let any of these terrific men get away!

Starting in January 1993   Price: £1.75

Available from Boots, Martins, John Menzies, W.H. Smith, most supermarkets and other paperback stockists.

Also available from Mills & Boon Reader Service, PO Box 236, Thornton Road, Croydon, Surrey CR9 3RU.
(UK Postage & Packing free)